MY HUSBAND'S SECRET

KIERSTEN MODGLIN

www.kierstenmodglinauthor.com
Cover Design: Tadpole Designs
Editing: Three Owls Editing
Proofreading: My Brother's Editor
Formatting: Tadpole Designs
First Print Edition: 2020
First Electronic Edition: 2020

To the hot tea drinkers out there—
my sisters in soul and steam

"We all have stories we won't ever tell."

CHAPTER ONE

NAOMI

Today would change everything.

Nothing would ever be the same.

The sky was as dark and stormy as the clouds I felt looming in my heart. I climbed from the car with a belly full of apprehension. Opening the back door, I pried my daughter's cheek from the drool-covered car seat strap. "Becca, wake up, sweetheart," I said, lifting her carefully from her seat. "We're here." I clutched the child to my chest, one hand placed on the back of her neck.

Her tiny body stirred in my arms. She smacked her lips together in her sleep and rolled her head to the other side. She mumbled something, not awake, and yet not completely asleep. I placed my cheek against hers.

There was no point in waking her up, I decided. Given any choice at all, I myself would've slept through this dreadful day.

I glanced down at the soggy grass, the leaves of fall sticking to my best black heels. In the distance, I could see the blue tent they'd put up to shield his casket. There seemed to be no one around, not that it surprised me entirely. Lucas wasn't exactly social or well-liked, even with all that he did for our little community. All that *I* did, via Lucas, anyway.

I brushed a bit of my chestnut hair back out of my face as the wind began to pick up and pulled my daughter in closer to my chest. I should've packed her a heavier jacket, but it hadn't seemed that cold when we first left the house. That was a Tennessee fall for you. You could never tell what to expect.

Then again, maybe I'd just become numb to it all. The weather, what to wear, what to say. How to live. It all felt a bit pointless. Losing a husband, I guessed, would do that to you.

When we finally reached the tent, I was soaked up to my ankles in freezing cold water, my legs already shaking from my daughter's weight. It killed me how big she was getting. I could vividly remember the days when she could almost completely fit in Lucas' palms, and now, she was nearly half the length of me. Death made one intro-spective, I was realizing. More sentimental thoughts came to me than ever before, washing over me with a vengeance that begged to be acknowledged. Dealt with. Pain that demanded to be felt.

My husband was dead.

My daughter was growing.

Soon enough, I'd be alone.

As I reached the casket, I made eye contact with the pastor. He was rather short and plump, with wild, gray eyebrows and freckles across his nose. His gray hair had been slicked to the side, so caked with gel it looked as though it wouldn't move in a hurricane. He offered me a small smile, his lips purple and thin in the cold. I didn't know him, except for our brief meeting at the funeral home. Lucas wasn't religious and I had my doubts about spirituality as well, so we'd never looked into a church. I guess you don't think about those things until you need them.

I'd opted for a closed casket—though I hadn't really been given a choice. His body wasn't in a state to be seen. With all the damage, it would be too much for me to see him like this. Too much for Becca especially. Instead, we remembered him through the oversized photo sitting on an easel beside the casket, a photo he would've chosen himself. He was smiling in it, warm and friendly like he'd done so many days in the beginning. He was charming then, and still after, but only when he needed to be. Becca stirred in my arms, bringing me back to reality. She was still too young to understand it—any of it. She kept asking for him, wondering when he'd be back home with us. I wondered if she'd remember him in the long run. There would be pictures, of course, and videos. I would tell her stories of her father and all of the goodness he brought to our lives, but I wouldn't tell her the bad.

She didn't need to know about the darkness.

It didn't matter anymore anyway.

I glanced up, noticing someone else approaching the gravesite. The intruder was a woman, though not one I recognized. She was tall and rail-thin, a jarring contradiction to everything about me. She held a cigarette between two claw-like fingers, blowing smoke into the breeze. I put a hand over Becca's face, stepping further away despite the already large amount of distance between us.

Though it was cloudy out, she was wearing large sunglasses, her tan legs shaking from the cold, and her lack of leggings. I would've felt almost bad for her, she was obviously distraught, but I couldn't focus any further than the burning questions swirling through my mind: who was she? How had she known my husband?

I watched the last bit of white on her cigarette burn orange before she tossed it to the wet ground, the stale smell carrying toward me as the wind's direction changed. She made her way up toward the casket with shaking hands, placing an outstretched palm on the oak I picked out. I looked around, wondering briefly if it was possible she had wandered up to the wrong burial, but there were no other services being performed in this cemetery today. Slowly, a group of others—mostly people Lucas had worked with at the hospital—began trickling in under the tent. I spotted a few familiar faces offering up sympathetic smiles. Some of the newcomers spoke to the blonde. It was obvious then that she was one of them. Someone who'd worked with Lucas. From the looks of it, someone who'd cared about him very much.

When the incoming traffic had come to a halt, we stood under the tent in silence, staring at the pastor, the solemn man who would say the final words before my husband and the secrets he was taking with him were placed in the ground for good.

All in all, there were fewer than ten of us. It was almost worse than there being none.

"Are we ready to get started?" the pastor asked under his breath, his eyes locked on mine.

I nodded without thinking. How was I supposed to answer that? How would I ever feel ready to say goodbye to my husband?

He cleared his throat, not reading the worry on my face, and moved to address the small crowd. "Thank you all for coming today. I know Naomi and the family really appreciate the support on what is going to be a hard day for us all." He opened the Bible in his hands and glanced back at me. *A hard day for us all.* Well, that was just the understatement of the year, wasn't it? My guess was, most of the people would head out to dinner after this or go back to work without a care in the world. Their lives would go on. They could imagine laughing again. They could breathe without the debilitating pain I felt at the mere thought of tomorrow. Next week. Next year.

What was the point of any of it without him?

Lucas meant nothing to his coworkers, his friends, compared to how I loved him. It wasn't a hard day. It was the worst day of my life. No one else understood that.

"Lucas Martin was a loving husband and father, a devoted surgeon, and a trusted member of the Nolensville community. He was…"

The words slammed into my chest, causing me to take a half-step back, and I inhaled sharply.

Lucas *was.*

Lucas is no longer.

I stopped listening, letting the words turn to a soft lull in my ears as something to my left caught my attention. I turned my head slightly, staring off toward where I was parked. A woman with raven, pixie-cut hair was rushing forward, her black trench coat flying out behind her as her boots hurried across the soggy ground. When she grew closer, slowing her steps so she could sneak in without disturbing the ceremony, I was immediately in awe of her beauty. Large, round eyes with carefully drawn brows and winged eyeliner; full, brown lips; and a hint of bronzer to accentuate her already high cheekbones. I couldn't help staring at her. There was something oddly familiar about her, but I couldn't place it. Who was she? How did she know Lucas?

Though most of the attendees were practically strangers, I, at least, recognized them. But these two women, the blonde and the brunette, were unknown to me. How was it possible, then, that they both had fresh tears in their eyes over my husband's passing?

Becca stirred in my arms, bringing me back to reality, and I began to bounce with her as I hadn't done since she was an infant. I needed her to stay calm, stay asleep. We just needed to get through the day, through that moment, and then I swore to myself everything would be okay.

No.

Everything would be *better*.

AFTER THE CEREMONY ENDED, people began to retreat to their cars almost immediately. A few gave Becca and me swift hugs and kind words. One woman asked if she could have a meal sent to our home. I accepted their condolences with grace but denied the meal. Cooking was the one thing that kept me sane, so I was happy to prepare our meals.

To my surprise, the two strange women didn't leave with the others. The raven-haired beauty stood back at the edge of the tent, wiping her hands across her cheeks as the tears fell. The blonde was inching closer and closer toward the casket, her eyes swimming with tears, though she made no move to dry them. She pulled another cigarette from the pocket of her sweater, her hands shaking as she lifted the lighter to the end.

I shielded Becca from the smoke, huffing. "Do you mind?" I asked.

She looked confused for a moment, then shoved the cigarette back into her pocket. "I'm sorry, I didn't think. I...um..." She put a hand to her lips, her voice gravelly from smoking. Finally, she said, "I'm Clara. You must be Naomi."

I nodded, surprised that she knew me when I had no idea who she was. "Uh, yes. Yes, I am."

"I'm...I'm so sorry for your loss," she said, her voice powerless.

"Thank you. Um, h-how did you know Lucas?"

She folded one arm across her body as if she were overcome with a chill. "We worked together."

"At the hospital? Are you a nurse?"

"A *doctor*," she corrected, making me feel like a terrible feminist. "Surgeon. Like Luke."

Luke. I'd always hated that shortening of my husband's name. "I'm sorry," I said.

"It's okay. And I know I shouldn't be smoking. I haven't in a few years, actually, but...I needed it today."

Her eyes were cold then. Distant. As if she had something else she wanted to say. There was a weight to her shoulders I hadn't noticed before. After a silent moment, she sighed, and the emotion evaporated from her face.

"I'm not sure any of the usual rules apply today." I paused, a shiver running over me. "Were you two close, then? You and Lucas?"

More tears filled her eyes as I nodded toward his casket. "You didn't know...I thought he'd—" It wasn't a question. Her lips were pressed into a thin line of confirmation. Didn't know what? She waved a hand at me. "It doesn't matter now, but I thought he'd told you about me. We'd...we'd been dating for about twelve years."

Her sentence took the wind straight out of me, and I moved a step backward. "You were...*dating* my...my husband?" I asked, my face wrinkled with confusion. Surely I'd just heard her wrong. It wasn't possible.

Her jaw dropped, but before she could answer, the woman in the corner stepped toward us, interrupting. "Hold on a second," she said, tears still falling as her voice turned from grief to confusion. "You were *both* seeing Lucas? *This* Lucas?" She gestured toward the oversized portrait of him next to the casket.

I scoffed. "I wasn't *seeing* him, I was *married* to him. What concern is it of yours?" I demanded, rage bubbling in my belly. "Who are you, anyway?" My body trembled with anger as I stared between the two women, both of them doing the same as we sized each other up.

She shook her head in disbelief. "I'm Alaina. We...we were engaged," the woman said, her voice trembling as she spoke. She placed her thin, pale fingers over her lips, and I wondered for a split second if she were going to be sick. "I knew he'd lied to me when I saw the obituary. I knew he had a wife, but…he was cheating on me with two women?" She clutched her chest, looking down as she swiped fresh tears from her eyes. A diamond ring glistened on her finger. "I can't believe this…"

"He wasn't cheating on *you*," I argued. "He was cheating on me…with *you!* I'm his wife. I'm the one who should be upset!"

"I didn't know about either of you," Clara said, stepping out of the triangle we'd unintentionally formed. Her face had gone ashen, the little bit of life left in her a moment ago appeared to have been zapped. "Honestly."

I looked at her, my heart pounding in my chest. It was entirely possible that I was going to pass out at any moment. Lucas couldn't have been cheating on me. I would've known. I would've sensed it, wouldn't I? I had access to everything—his phone, our bank accounts. I wasn't just a complacent spouse. I knew everything. We had no secrets.

Not anymore.

I'd discovered them.

Figured them out and taken care of them.

He knew better than to hide anything from me.

And yet, apparently, he had. He'd kept secrets so big they could ruin everything, and they were staring at me, waiting for me to answer the questions in their eyes.

"You knew about me, though," I said finally, looking directly at Clara. "You knew my name. Who I was."

"Yes. I…uh, I knew about you." She blinked slowly. "But not about your relationship. He told me he had a sister named Naomi who lived with him," she said. "I assumed that was you. He said he was helping to raise her daughter. It wasn't until the pastor said husband and father that I began to realize I didn't know that much about him at all." A shadow cast over her expression again as she shifted in place. "Luke was good at keeping secrets. I just never realized they'd be this big."

"A-a *sister?*" I couldn't believe it, though the truth was there in her eyes. "He said I was his *sister?* He said Becca wasn't his…" I lowered my voice as I watched the pastor growing nearer to our tent, having said goodbye to the final guest. "His daughter?"

"I'm so sorry," she said, watching me stagger backward. "Do you want me to take her?" She gestured toward Becca who was beginning to wake in my arms as my knees shook under our weight. The whole world went blurry as I tried to process what I was being told. It was impossible.

"Don't touch my daughter," I said angrily, jerking her back from Clara's reaching grasp.

"I can't believe that bastard did this to us," Alaina said.

"Language!" I chided. Becca's eyes were open then, and she stared around.

"Mommy?" she asked. "Where are we?"

"Is everything all right?" the pastor asked.

Alaina rolled her eyes and flicked her wrist. "I just want to see him and say goodbye. None of this matters anymore anyway, does it?"

"He was my husband," I said through bared teeth, my eyes flicking toward the pastor as I ignored the question, still consumed with what I was discovering. "This is my life. Of course, it matters."

She held up her hand, giving us a better look at a ring that was twice the size of mine. My heart stopped, my veins going ice cold. "He was my fiancé. We were getting married next year. It's my life too, okay?" The tears were back as she pressed her lips to her knuckles.

"Next year? He was *still* married to me," I said, shaking my head. It felt like a cruel prank. My jaw tensed, my whole body rife with venom as I willed myself to calm down, though it was hardly any use.

"It's okay, Mommy," Becca said, her tiny hands on my cheeks as my tears began to fall. "It's okay." She had always loved to comfort me.

"How did you even meet him?" Clara asked Alaina. "You don't work at the hospital."

"He goes to other places besides the hospital," I snipped, my hands shaking, though I had no idea why I was arguing that point.

"My grandmother was one of his patients," Alaina said, ignoring me. "Not that I owe either of you any explanations." She paused. "We met two years ago during one of her last surgeries. After she died…Lucas was the only one who was there for me."

"Two years ago?" Clara asked, anger in her feeble voice for what seemed like the first time. "We've been dating twelve years, and *you're* the one he proposed to? What the hell have you got that I don't?"

"None of the engagements matter because he couldn't be married to either of you," I cut in, anger seething in my belly. "Lucas was *my* husband. He was Becca's father. Now, I don't know what promises he made to either of you, what lies he fed you, but today is his funeral. I'd appreciate it if you would both just leave so I can grieve with my child. We need to say goodbye."

Clara's eyes shot toward Alaina, and she frowned. "I'd like to say goodbye, too," she said.

"Me too," Alaina agreed. She looked at me. "I'll make it quick."

Without waiting for permission, Alaina approached the head of the casket. She leaned across it, and I couldn't help picturing her draped across my husband in the same way. A tear cascaded down her cheek and onto the wood. "I love you," she whispered, kissing the top with her eyes closed. I forced myself to look away, my vision blurring with fury.

When she lifted up, Clara quickly replaced her. Her sobs were loud and obnoxious as she fell over the casket. Alaina walked past me without a word, and I watched Clara fall apart, her cries carrying through the quiet cemetery.

"Would you wrap it up please?" I asked, staring at Becca's worried expression as she watched the show. I couldn't believe this was happening.

Clara stood, walking away from the casket as she wiped her hand under her dripping nose. "I'm so sorry, Naomi." I pressed my lips together. What was I supposed to say? It was okay? Nothing about this was okay.

Without another word, she was gone, headed back to her car, and I was left alone with Becca, Lucas' casket, the confused-looking pastor, and an enormous amount of secrets.

I walked with trepidation toward the box that housed my husband's body. I was still grieving, of course, but there were new feelings filling me now. Confusion. Anger. Heartbreak of a new kind.

"How could you have done this to us?" I asked, my voice a low whisper.

"What did I do, Mommy?" my daughter asked, touching my cheek again and pulling my face to look at her.

I smiled, twirling a finger through one of her spiral curls. "Nothing at all, sweetheart."

"Where's Daddy?" she asked, and I watched her eyes as they locked onto the blown-up photograph of Lucas on our left.

"Daddy's gone, baby," I told her with a kiss on her cheek. "But he'll always be with us." The knots in my stomach tightened as I realized just how true that was. The repercussions of my husband's choices, his mistakes, I had a feeling, would haunt me for the rest of my life.

CHAPTER TWO

CLARA

I walked into the apartment with a lit cigarette in my mouth. It had been so long since I'd allowed myself such an indulgence. Luke always hated the smell, and my years of medical practice told me of the damage it was causing, but something deep inside of me still craved it on hard days.

Today was an especially hard day.

Meeting Naomi for the first time, discovering the truth about all that Luke had lied about—keeping in the truth of what I had to lie about—it was all that I could do to hold it together. And I *had* to hold it together.

I was due at the hospital soon for two back-to-back surgeries, but I'd overestimated my abilities. When I received the news of Luke's funeral, I lost it. God, I lost it. Somehow, learning that he was going to be buried made it all real.

When we met, back when I started my internship and he was already a bright, young surgeon a few years younger than I was, I thought he was a pretentious asshole. As I got to know him more, I realized it was completely true. But he was also charming and incredibly kind.

He didn't judge me for starting medical school twenty years later than the rest of my class. He told me he was proud of me. Said it was brave to start out later in life. He walked me through my first surgery when I froze up— refused to help, and insisted I could do it on my own. And, of course, he was right. I did it.

It was one of my fondest memories of him—him teaching me to go for it on my own. Little did I know, he was preparing me for a future without him.

How dare you? How dare you do this to me?

I fell to the floor of our living room in agony, the rough carpet scraping my knees and elbows. Everything in our apartment was a reminder of him. The couch he helped me pick out, the curtains he'd helped hang, the kitchen counter from where we'd shoved a cookie sheet to the floor while we were making love just a few short weeks ago.

It wasn't fair. None of it was fair. My emotions were so conflicted as I ran my hands through the carpet of my home, my body shaking with silent sobs. I thought the worst thing I'd ever experience would be losing him, but I was wrong. Finding out he betrayed me, that he'd lied about so much while having no place to displace that anger, that was what hurt the most. I'd heard before that grief is just love with no place to go. I wondered if they had a word for fury with the same problem. I wanted to be mad at him, I wanted to hate him…but what good would it do? It wouldn't affect anyone but me at that point.

I was not sure I knew who I was without Luke. He was such a huge part of my life for twelve years. Hell, if I were being honest, aside from surgery, he *was* my whole life for twelve years.

Now, he was gone, and I was left to figure out how to feel about him and myself, and this whole other life he was living. *Two* other lives.

How could I have been so blind to his lies? When I'd caught him in a lie the first time, I should've walked away. But I believed him. I believed him when he said he loved me. I believed him when he said he'd never lie again. I believed him when he said everything was going to be okay.

But nothing was okay.

Nothing would ever be okay again.

Luke wasn't to blame for the worst of it, though. I knew that. Still, it didn't ease the pain I felt.

How much of what I believed about the man I loved was a lie?

CHAPTER THREE

ALAINA

I didn't want to believe it. Any of it. When I first met Lucas, he was the surgeon responsible for my grand-mother's tumor removal. That was it. He was handsome, sure. And I saw the way he looked me over, but I was used to that.

From the time I was a teenager, men had always given me a second glance. It was nothing new and nothing that seemed to be going away any time soon.

When my grandmother passed away, I was surprised to receive flowers at work from Lucas, but I assumed they were technically from the hospital. Then, a few weeks later, he called me to check in and see how I was getting on. Not well, if I were being honest, and though I tried to pretend everything was fine, he seemed to see right through it.

He was like that, you know? He could read right into whatever you said, cutting through to your true feelings. He was impulsive and ill-tempered, but he was also the kind of man who went all out on our anniversary without having to be reminded.

He was the kind of person who, when we left to go anywhere, asked how long I thought it would take. He was always in a hurry, though we had no real place to be. When we went shopping, he went straight to the places we needed to be. He wasn't a browser. I'd never seen him do anything leisurely. He moved with intent, acted with passion. So, he loved with both.

I couldn't think of him without recalling the good times—the ones in the beginning. For our first date, he'd taken me axe throwing. He took one look at my combat boots and black clothing and thought, *"I'll bet she loves to throw weapons."* I remember laughing at how well he knew me when we pulled up to the date. I pretended the whole night that it was my first time, and I let Lucas show me up. He loved to seem stronger than he was. He always wanted to be in control.

After that first date, our dates mostly consisted of eating takeout on my floor, watching old horror films, and laughing our asses off at the bad special effects. We'd never finished a single film, always ending the night with food on the floor and our clothes strewn about while we made love wherever we were. We rarely made it to the bed—didn't need to.

He understood a side of me that no one else did, and he tapped into it. He broke down my walls, walls that had been built by a terrible relationship with my own father and even worse relationships with men in general. Lucas was different, I thought. When he'd looked at me, it was as if nothing else mattered.

I thought nothing else had.

Now, though, knowing that he had loved other women in the same way—I wasn't sure where that left me. I wasn't his wife yet. Wasn't ever going to be now. In fact, given that he *had* a wife, it seemed impossible that I would've ever been.

Did it make me regret my decisions? No.

Did it make me worry that the truth might come out? More than ever.

There were two others involved now, two others who'd be determined to know the truth, maybe even more than the police.

I placed a careful hand over my belly, over the small bump we had formed there.

"No one can take you away from me, little one," I promised the bump, the only piece of Lucas I had left. No matter what I found out about him in the future, no matter what had happened in our past, he loved me enough to plan a future with me, to propose, and to celebrate the news of my pregnancy. Our love was different. I had to believe that. Even if it was built on lies, when he told me he loved me, I had to believe he meant it. If not, everything I'd done had been for nothing. Two years of my life wasted. I wouldn't allow myself to believe that. Lucas loved me, and he loved our child. At least, that was the story I was going to spin.

CHAPTER FOUR

NAOMI

The first time I met Lucas, I was ready to die. It sounds dramatic, I know, and I guess it is. But he saved me.

Okay, as it turns out—as he would inform me later—it wasn't the *first* time we met. I didn't remember him before then, I still don't understand how, but we actually went to the same university and even had a few of the same classes. He was three years ahead of me.

But, as it stands, according to my own memory, the first time I met the man with whom I meant to spend my life, I was planning to end it.

I mean, I wasn't standing on a bridge or anything. I wasn't that close. But I'd made the decision. I think most people believe suicide is an impulse. That you have a bad day and make a bad decision. But that's not the case. At least, it wasn't for me.

I'd become obsessed with death. I'd done the research, hoarded the pills. It would be painless from all that I'd read. I'd written letters to my parents and my older sister. I'd picked the day and the time that it would be done.

But Lucas approached me one day as he was jogging through the park. I'd gone there to clear my head. I was just two days away from my death, and the fear had begun to creep in.

I swear somehow he knew my plan, though he'd deny it to this day if he was still around to do that. He walked up to me, him with his coal-black hair and dark eyes, me with my ratty hair tied back into a bun because I couldn't bring myself to brush it anymore. He was beautiful where I was plain; he was articulate where words failed me; he was charming while I remained awkward. I was not the type of girl he should've been coming up to. I was convinced he must've been waiting for someone else. When he sat, I stood. Like a teeter-totter, as his butt hit the bench, mine was up.

"I'm sorry." I heard his apology, and then he was standing too. "I didn't mean to disturb you."

I looked back at him then, and he smiled. *Oh, I remember his smile.* Warmth all the way up to his eyes.

"Y-you didn't...disturb me." I hadn't heard my own voice in so long it felt foreign. No one expected to hear me talk, so I didn't have any use for it. My parents were in Rome, and my professors didn't push any harder to hear from those of us who didn't raise our hands. I was allowed to maintain my silence, but finally, someone was asking me to speak.

"I'm Lucas," he said, reaching out his hand.

"Naomi," I told him my name. "Nice run?" I asked because I could think of nothing else to say.

He nodded, pulling the remaining earbud from his ear. "It's a beautiful day for one." He looked back toward the bench. "Were you…waiting for someone?"

I shook my head. "No. I was just…" I trailed off, unable to finish the sentence. What the heck was I trying to think of anyway?

"Would you like to join me?" He seemed to understand that I wasn't planning to finish that thought.

"Oh," I glanced down at my jeans. "I'm not really dressed for it." I waved my hand casually to let him know I was fine.

"We can walk," he said. "I'm in no hurry."

I smiled then, and the expression felt strange to my facial muscles. I still don't know what it was about me that made him come to where I was that day, but I was so thankful he did. As a surgeon, my husband saved countless lives every day at work, but he'd tell me he was always the proudest of the only life he ever saved without a scalpel. Mine.

Thinking of him made my heart ache. During the bustle of the day, between taking care of Becca and trying to restart my old interior design business, I could somewhat easily put my thoughts and feelings aside, but during the evening, once Becca was down for the night, that was when the pain began to seep through the cracks.

Three nights had passed since Lucas' funeral, and I still felt like I was living my life in a fog. Becca still hadn't grasped it, and every time she asked about her father, my heart broke a little more. Any piece that may have felt repaired shattered once again.

I picked up my phone without planning to, scrolling

through my contacts. I knew it was a mistake as soon as I saw his name, but I couldn't help myself. I didn't want to help myself. I was lonely. I needed to talk to someone. Anyone.

I should've called anyone else, but no one else could fill the hole that Lucas' death had left.

He picked up on the second ring. "Everything all right?"

"Yes," I said, stifling a sob. "No." I put a hand on my chest. "I just...need you."

He was quiet, so quiet I almost wondered if he hung up on me, but then I heard him sigh. "Naomi, I can't."

"I know," I said, wiping my tears.

"You shouldn't have called me."

"I know."

"I mean, your husband just died. It's going to look suspicious if you start having anyone coming around at night, but especially me. We have to be smart about this."

I sniffled, pulling my knees up to my chest. "I'm sorry, it was stupid."

The anger in his voice faded quickly. "It's not stupid... You know I would be there in a second if I could. I hate being away from you."

"It hurts more than I ever thought possible," I told him. He was the only person I could truly be honest with. "Losing him... Missing you. Trying to keep it together after what happened. I'm so scared...and sad. I've never hurt like this."

He huffed, and I could picture him running his hands through his hair. "I'm sorry, Naomi. I wish there was something I could do, I really do."

"I know."

He took another breath. "Are you going to be okay?"

"I will be. Eventually."

"It's going to get better," he said. "Once things calm down some, we can see each other again."

"I wish you were here now," I told him, fat tears filling my vision again.

"So do I. More than you know." It wasn't technically true. I did know. I knew how much he missed me. How much he wanted to protect me. I knew he felt powerless over all of this.

What I didn't know was how he could still love me knowing the truth about what I'd done.

CHAPTER FIVE

CLARA

"Clara? Clara, what are you doing?" The voice was low and unrecognizable, and I wondered who was in my bedroom, but not enough to wake. I rubbed a finger across my face, my body unmoving as I felt myself falling back to sleep.

"Clara?" There it was again, and this time I startled, opening one eye and then the other.

The room I'd been asleep in wasn't my bedroom.

I blinked the sleep from my eyes and sat up.

"What?" I asked quietly, sucking in a deep breath. "Where am—" I stopped, because the answer came to me nearly as quickly as the question.

The supply room.

At work.

I lifted myself from the floor as the memories came back to me.

Luke's dead.

He's gone.

I'll never see him again.

I can't do this.

"Are you okay? Are you hurt?" I had no *true* work friends, now that Luke was gone, but Elizabeth was the next closest thing. The attending surgeon reached for my head, looking me over. Her red waves were tied back in a low ponytail, a stunning contrast to the black scrubs she wore.

"I'm not hurt," I said. I didn't want her to know the truth, but as I answered, I saw her face registering the scent on my breath.

Her expression went blank, her green eyes instantly serious. "You've been drinking."

"I'm sorry," I said. I was holding a packet of gauze so tightly, when I opened my fist, it remained stuck to it. I peeled it from my skin and placed it back on the shelf. "I'll go talk to Cooper." I didn't want to talk to our boss, but anything was better than the pitiful look I was getting from her. "I need to go home."

She placed her hand on my shoulder, stopping me from walking away. "You didn't answer me."

I cocked my head to the side, asking an unspoken question.

"Are you okay?" she asked again, this time slowly, taking her time with each word. Her eyes crinkled at the sides, proving she knew more than she was letting on. Luke and I were quiet about our relationship. A few people knew, but it wasn't something we flaunted. Looking back, I realized it was likely because he was trying to keep me a secret, but at the time it made sense not wanting to be too bold with our status. We wanted our careers to be viewed separately from each other. I wanted people to take me seriously as a surgeon. Though I was older, Luke was more accomplished. I'd already seen how being a man gave him an unfair advantage, even if we'd had a level playing field, which we never did. I didn't want anyone to think that any success I achieved was owed to him.

"No," I said finally, shoving past her on my way out of the storage room. My success wasn't thanks to Luke, but it was possible the downfall of my career would be. I was not okay. In fact, I was not sure I'd ever be okay without him.

What have I done?

CHAPTER SIX

ALAINA

I was standing in front of a familiar house four times the size of my tiny apartment with wide eyes and my heart racing wild in my chest. The message on my phone made me nervous, but ignoring it would be worse. I needed to know what Naomi wanted to know—what Lucas' *wife* wanted to know.

Wife.

The thought was a knife to the heart, ripping and stabbing what was left of my resolve. Not only had I lost the man I loved, the father of the child growing in my womb, but I'd found out he'd been lying to me for our entire relationship. Lying about more than I already knew he'd lied about. I didn't know what to do with the truth, so I'd tucked it away for now. I planned to deal with it later, but grief had to come first.

When Naomi sent me the Facebook message that morning, a huge part of me wanted to ignore it, but I couldn't. I knew I couldn't the moment I read it.

The police are asking questions about Lucas' death. I

need to know if I should tell them about your involvement with him. We should talk. Can you come to my house at one this afternoon?

She included her address and I drove by it right away, but a drive-by didn't do justice to pulling in the drive just now. It was incredible, all brown brick, two stories, with large windows and black shutters to match the front door, and an expansive front lawn with freshly mown lines. I couldn't picture Lucas here. Not the man I knew. The man who ate Chinese takeout straight from the carton on my living room floor and drank cheap beer with me. The man who pulled off his tie the moment he arrived in my doorway and talked to me about art and foreign films. He wasn't materialistic, the man I loved, but the man who lived in this house obviously was. I was finding it impossible to believe they were one and the same.

I walked up the front lawn toward the door but stopped when I realized there was another woman standing in the shaded space before the front door, nearly hidden in the shadows. She swayed when she saw me, glancing over her shoulder. Tall, blonde, and incredibly skinny, she was beautiful for her age, which was probably double mine. I couldn't remember her name, but I knew who she was. *Lucas'*...what, exactly? Girlfriend, I guess. She'd said she was dating Lucas for...twelve years. Just under half my life, but I was the one he'd chosen to marry. I was the one carrying his child. I had to believe I was the one he loved.

"Alaina?" she asked, her voice deep and scarred from cigarettes. She'd been smoking just before she arrived, I'd bet, based on the scent that carried past me on the wind.

I nodded, stepping up next to her. "Hi."

"Clara," she reminded me of her name. "What are you doing here?"

"Same thing you are, I'm guessing." I jutted my chin toward the door. "Naomi contacted you, too?"

Her gaze faltered, obviously uncomfortable, and she looked back at the door. "What do you think she wants to know?"

"I know what I'd want to know...if the situation were reversed."

She waited for me to go on, but I didn't bother, though the questions I'd have—the questions I assumed she had—were still on my tongue. *Who killed my husband? Why did he choose you? Why wasn't I enough?* "Did you knock already?"

She nodded, looking away. The awkwardness in the air was palpable, and I couldn't help thinking, again, of the Lucas I knew so well. How could he have loved someone like Clara and someone like me the same? We were totally different. Clara looked tired and worn, while I was full of life. The fake tan she was sporting was sure to eventually give her cancer if the diet soda in her hand didn't manage to first. Her boobs were fake, her teeth too white. I didn't understand. How could he look at us and feel anything similar?

The door finally swung open and the woman from the funeral stood in front of us. Naomi Martin. While Lucas claimed he hadn't *believed* in social media, over the past week, I'd come to find out his wife did. Since the funeral, I'd spent many nights flipping between her Facebook albums—she wasn't on Instagram—to catch a glimpse of what her life looked like with Lucas. *My* Lucas. But also hers. Also Clara's.

"Hi," Naomi said, pulling me from my thoughts. She was dressed in a simple black top and jeans, a high ponytail holding her chestnut brown hair back. "Good. You're both here. Thank you, ladies, for coming." She stepped back from the door and held her arm out. "Come in, please."

Clara stepped through first, and I watched her steps slow as we made it across the threshold and into the home. The first room was a simple foyer with white, marble floors, and a curved set of stairs against the wall to our left led upstairs. Naomi led us to the left and past the stairs to a living room with high, vaulted ceilings and floor-to-ceiling drapes in a deep auburn color. The floors in this room were a stained ebony-brown hardwood straight from the magazines, but my eye was immediately drawn to the large, black and white canvases with family portraits of them. They were beautiful together, Lucas, Naomi, and their baby girl, who I'd gathered from Facebook to be named Rebecca. He looked happy, the smile he wore was undeniable, and there was no stiffness to the way he was with her.

It hurt more than seeing it online because, here, it was real. He lived here within these walls with her. He may have even hung the pictures I was staring at. It took the breath from my lungs to look over them, and I felt as though I might pass out.

"Please, sit," Naomi instructed, right on time, walking past us and taking a seat on a gray armchair with dark brown legs. Clara sat across from her on the matching gray sofa, while I took the recliner at the far side of the room, keeping my sweater pulled away from my belly. I didn't want them to notice the bump. I couldn't handle it yet.

Naomi watched me with a stiff, almost pained expression, and the moment I sat, I realized why. *The chair smells like him.* The smell of his mint and bergamot cologne hit me all at once, and I felt tears sting my eyes. I wanted to hold him. It was an embarrassing realization while sitting across from his wife and other girlfriend...lover, whatever she was, but it was still there, and I couldn't shy away from it. I wanted to see him again, to kiss him. To be with him.

There was a tray with three empty glasses and a pitcher of cucumber water on a white, marble coffee table in front of us, and Naomi scooted toward the front of her seat, gesturing toward the pitcher. "Would you like anything to drink?"

Fat chance. I'd learned my lesson about drinking anything I didn't prepare myself. "I'm okay."

At the same time, Clara said, "Please." She cleared her throat for the hundredth time as Naomi poured her a glass, then she poured one for herself. She took a sip, letting it settle on her tongue before she began.

"So, I know you probably weren't expecting to hear from me. If I'm being honest, I had hoped I wouldn't have to hear or think about either of you again."

I couldn't tell if she was being polite or verbally assaulting us. Her expression was still and cool, yet her tone was warm.

"But, I'm afraid this couldn't wait. I know we all probably have questions about Lucas…about what he meant to each of us and how exactly he made…" she gestured to each of us, "*this* work, but right now my main concern is to get answers about what happened the day he died."

Her words sat squarely on my gut, and I swallowed. A cold sweat formed on my brow. *What does she mean? What does she know? What is she asking?*

"The police are still treating his death as suspicious, and…if either of you know anything, I'd…well, I'd really like to know." She brushed a stray tear away from the corner of her eye, the shell she was hiding behind disappearing all at once. "I'd like to be able to give my daughter some answers about what happened to her father one day."

"Are you asking if…we… What? If we killed him?" I asked, venom in my tone. Was she serious?

"Of course not," she said. "I'd just like to know what happened. What was going on with him on the day that he died. Where his head was. If it was an accident, or God forbid, suicide, then so be it. But if there's more to it…the police would like to know, and frankly, so would I. Had either of you seen him that day? That week? Is there anything you can tell me about what might've been going through his mind? Maybe he'd been having trouble with a patient…or someone else? Is there anything suspicious you can think of at all?" She ran her hands over her knees. "I just want to know the truth."

"The truth about what, Naomi? What do you think happened?" Clara asked, reaching for her hand across the table. She froze, pulling it back. "I'm sorry. I feel like I know you. Luke told me so much…" She trailed off, rubbing her finger across her bottom lip. "It's not my place."

"*Lucas* lied to us all about…" Naomi rolled her eyes, batting back tears. "About so much. I don't want all of the truth. I'm…not sure I can handle all of it, but I'd like to know enough to get the police to close the case. To put this to bed so my family and I can move on." She sniffled, rubbing a finger under her nose delicately. "As far as I know, the police don't know anything about either of you, but if you can help them, help us… Well, it would be very appreciated. If you loved Lucas like I assume you did, we all want the same thing, right? I just want to know the truth of what happened."

Clara took another sip of her water, sitting back as we each waited for anyone else to speak first. We each had secrets, that much was obvious. We had reasons to want Lucas' case to be closed. Whoever spoke first, it wouldn't be me. I had no idea what I wanted to say, other than nothing. I wanted the conversation to be over. I wanted to go home, where I was safe.

I swallowed, rubbing a hand over the small bump beneath my top without thought.

"Right now, the police don't know you two were involved with my husband. If we can resolve the matter between us, I don't see any reason to involve them. I know we're all hurting right now, and shocked, of course, but that's no reason we can't work together to get to the truth. Is it?" Naomi asked.

Clara cleared her throat, and I was sure she was going to begin to tell her version of things. "Maybe you should tell us what you know first. Just so we know…what happened between you two and where we need to fill in the blanks."

"What are you implying?" Naomi demanded.

"Nothing, of course. It's just… Well, we loved him too, like you said. I'd like to know the truth just as well as you would."

They both looked at me, waiting for me to agree. *The truth.* It was a funny thing, wasn't it?

CHAPTER SEVEN

NAOMI

Ten Days Before Lucas' Death

A hand slid over my torso, rousing me from sleep. I rolled over, one eye squeezed shut as I inhaled sharply. He pulled me into him, his fingers trailing across my skin toward my back.

"Good morning, beautiful."

I rubbed the messy, dark hair from his eyes. "Good morning." My voice was gruff with sleep, but he pressed his lips to mine, waking me up completely. "What's gotten into you this morning?"

He kissed me again, his lips fresh and minty. He smelled of soap; he'd already been in the shower. His eyes trailed across the room, and I followed them to where a tray of food sat on my dresser. The smile on my lips grew shamelessly.

"Happy Birthday," he whispered, reminding me. His face pressed into the side of mine. He kissed my temple. "I love you."

I rubbed my eyes, popping my back as I sat up. "Thank you, baby." He jumped from the bed and rushed across the room, grabbing the tray and carrying it toward me. "Where's Becca?"

"I didn't want to wake her."

I took a sip of my coffee, enjoying the perfect amount of caramel creamer. Lucas was always good about remembering just how I liked it. "You could've been a barista in another life, you know?"

He twisted a piece of the comforter between his fingers. "How do you know I wasn't?"

"Maybe you should be again," I teased. "You might be better at this than surgery."

"For my patients' sake, I hope not," he said with a snort, then sighed. "Maybe one day when we're living in the south of France, I'll open up a coffee shop."

"And we can live above it in a tiny apartment with a balcony," I said, playing along with the fantasy. "Of course, we'd have to summer back home where there's air conditioning."

He laughed. "Yes, of course. Our shop would only be open in the winter, and you could sit on the balcony every morning all snuggled in a blanket and smell my coffee brewing."

"*Or* you could just bring me a cup of coffee every morning. Then I wouldn't have to just smell it."

"I could do that here," he said, one brow raising. "And then we wouldn't have to worry about vandals destroying the shop in the summer. Can you imagine insurance on a vacant restaurant six months out of the year?"

"Fair enough. I guess France will just have to wait." I

giggled, taking another sip of the coffee. "What should we do today?"

"It's your day, gorgeous. What do you want to do?"

I stared at him incredulously. "You mean you don't have to work?"

He smiled with just one side of his mouth. "Just for a few hours. I've already told the chief I'm coming home early to spend it with my beautiful wife on her birthday."

"And Cooper was okay with that?"

He ran a hand down his side playfully. "When you look this good, you can get away with almost everything."

I rolled my eyes, setting my coffee down and lifting the tray to place it on my nightstand. "Prove it," I teased, turning back to him. His hands traveled up my waist, tickling my skin. *Hands of a surgeon*—every movement was precise and intentional as he spread the warmth of his palms across my bare skin.

"It'd be my pleasure," he whispered, connecting his lips with mine. The pit of my stomach tingled with desire as he shifted his weight on top of my body, his kisses growing fevered.

"Mommy?" Becca's tiny voice interrupted us, and Lucas rolled off me, breathing heavily.

"Good morning, pumpkin," I said, not missing a beat as I held out my arms for her. She watched us from where she stood in the hallway. I cast a silly glance at Lucas, who shook his head, an exasperated look on his face. He patted the cover on top of my tummy.

"Come wish Mommy a happy birthday, Bec," he said. At his invitation, she hurried across the room, bouncing up on top of me and giggling.

"Happy Birthday, Mommy," she cheered, bouncing up and down. Lucas pulled her over, kissing her forehead. "How old are you?"

"Old," I said with a laugh.

"You have to take care of her while Daddy's at work, okay? Deal?"

She twisted in his arms with glee. "Deal!"

He leaned forward, kissing my forehead. "Don't lift a finger today, you hear me? I have two surgeries this morning, both minor, but I'll be home right after."

I nodded, watching him leave the bed and then the room. I looked at Becca, who was snuggled into my arm, her brown curls messy from sleep.

"Want some breakfast?" I pulled the tray over onto the bed again. "Sit still, okay?" I warned as she sat up, fully prepared to devour the breakfast.

She clapped her hands together excitedly just as my phone chimed. "Okay!"

As she dug into the biscuit waiting for her, I reached for my phone, unplugging it and pulling it to me. Blinking and leaning my head back, I read the message on the screen.

My heart plummeted, chills running down my spine.

Happy Birthday.

Two words, one period. A seemingly simple message, but I knew it was far from simple. It had been a month since I'd talked to him, a month since we made a mistake I couldn't take back despite how badly I wanted to. The guilt of what happened weighed heavily on me and there had been countless times I'd considered telling Lucas, but how could I ever explain it? He'd never forgive me.

I deleted the text message, wishing I could delete what I'd done just as easily.

CHAPTER EIGHT

CLARA

"By the time we got in there, there was already so much damage from the blockage, the only option was a complete bowel resection, but the anastomosis went beautifully," I said, taking a bite of the turkey wrap in front of me. "How did your biopsy go?"

"The patient's a mess," he said, rubbing a hand over his chin. "But the surgery went well. We got a clean sample. Now we wait."

"Do you think it's…" I could tell by the look on his face that I didn't need to continue my sentence. The tests would only confirm what he and the rest of the surgical team already knew. The twenty-four-year-old science teacher had breast cancer, and her entire life was about to change.

It could all change so fast. That's what was so terrifying about our job. We tried so hard to protect, to save, to win, but it didn't always happen. And even when you'd won, even when we saved you, once you'd been on that table, you were never truly the same. Whether cancer or cesarean, the scalpel's scar tended to run deeper than the physical ones we left. As surgeons, the threat of our own mortality was constantly thrust in our faces. It could all be over just like that; everything could end.

I swallowed, no longer hungry, and dusted off my hands. "Are you coming over tonight?"

"I can't," he said simply, chewing on the last bit of crust from his pizza.

"Why not?"

He stood, dusting his hands off on his scrubs. "Today's Naomi's birthday. I promised her I'd cook dinner and watch Becca so she can relax."

I pursed my lips. "When am I going to get to meet this mysterious sister of yours? You know I'm great with kids." Or, at least I *would* be, if I had a chance to be around them.

"Soon," he promised, tapping the table with his knuckles, though his eyes were distant. That was how he was with this subject, one that had been brought up so often over the years. Never definitive. "You know Naomi is still fragile, and I just, I don't want to risk her health right now. Her doctors say she needs stability."

"I know," I said. I didn't want to push, even though the excuse fell flat. I believed Naomi must not like me, though I didn't know why. For twelve years, I'd dated her brother and never once had we been allowed to meet. Wasn't she curious about me? How much longer could he put it off? "I just...I want to help. I feel so useless here when you're doing so much."

"You help me," he confirmed. "You do, Clara. Just by being here...by being you." He squeezed my hand briefly, then turned away. "See you later."

"Bye," I called after him, tossing my napkin into the container on top of my lunch. I loved Luke, I really did, and I knew his heart was in the right place. There were few men I knew who would allow their sister to move in with them, let alone take care of both her and her daughter on top of maintaining a demanding full-time job. I didn't want to push. I knew he was balancing so much, and the last thing I wanted to do was ask for anything more.

I had my career too, something that meant so much to me. I could easily push aside any other worries. He loved me, I knew, and at least for now, we'd be together in whatever way he could make it work.

As long as I had him, in whatever capacity he could give himself to me, I wouldn't complain. We made that silent agreement years ago.

Still, I planned to meet Naomi one way or another. I was going to show Luke that everything would be okay between us. I'd make sure Naomi loved me. He'd see.

CHAPTER NINE

ALAINA

Someone was standing behind me. I sensed it in an instant, pulling the headphones from my ears and spinning around with my paintbrush wielded like a sword. Lucas looked back at me, obviously amused.

"Easy there, tiger," he teased, his hands thrown up in surrender. I groaned, rolling my eyes and lowering my brush.

"You scared me!"

He chuckled under his breath. "You didn't answer when I knocked. I assumed you were working and used the key."

I took off my apron and hung it on the side of the canvas stand, placing my paintbrush down. When I turned back to him, he was eyeing my painting as he pulled me into his arms for a quick kiss.

"What is this one about?"

"It's not *about* anything," I said with a sigh. "It's just...a feeling. My feelings."

He leaned a cheek onto the top of my head, squeezing me tighter. "And what are your feelings?"

I bit my tongue, not yet ready to talk about them. "Come with me. I finished up the one I've been working on this week, and I've been dying to show you."

He didn't seem fazed by the sudden change of subject, and as I tugged his hand down the long hallway toward my bedroom, he followed. Lucas had always been supportive of my art, even when he didn't completely understand it. He attended every one of my art shows and had even purchased a few pieces for himself. One day, when we had our own place together, he swore it would be filled with my art.

I pushed open the bedroom door and flipped on the light, tugging the white cover off the canvas in the corner. We stepped around the paintings that were wrapped and ready to be sent off to a buyer, and I watched Lucas' face change from amused to amazed.

He stepped past me, his fingers lifting to the canvas, though he dared not touch it. He sucked in a sharp breath. "Wow…this is…wow."

He stared at the charcoal and watercolor portrait of himself, taking in the lines I'd been meticulous about. Every inch of his body, as it was burned into my mind, was now on the canvas and preserved forever.

"Do you like it?" I asked when he'd been silent too long.

He nodded. "It's…me."

I laughed, shocked by his obvious words. "Yes, it's you."

He glanced over his shoulder at me, an awe-filled expression on his face. "When did you do this?"

"I've been working on it for a few weeks now, just here and there. I wanted it to be perfect."

"Are you...selling it?" He suddenly looked uncomfortable.

"Not a chance. This one's all mine."

He warmed instantly. "And when do I get one of *you*?" His fingers outstretched for my waist, and he pulled me toward him. I grinned.

"So you do like it, then?"

"It's beautiful."

"*You're* beautiful, Lukey," I said, nudging my nose against his as he lowered his lips to mine. I closed my eyes, sinking into his kiss as his arms wrapped around me, his leg bumping mine as he led me backward three steps and onto the bed.

He sank down on top of me, careful that his weight wasn't on my belly as his hand crawled up to my breast. His other hand cupped my jaw, pulling me into his kiss even more. He was such a good kisser, so much better than the many guys I dated in college. It was one of my favorite things about dating a much older man. On top of his maturity, he was incredibly experienced, and he put all that experience to good use with me.

He pulled away, staring down at me for a brief second. "You remembered every inch of me. Down to the freckles on my hip."

"You're burned into my memory, Lucas Martin. Deal with it." I beamed. "Artist brain is a very real thing."

"I guess I have some memorizing of my own to do." His eyebrows bounced up with desire as he pulled my dress over my head, his heated gaze raking over my body.

Remember me how I am now, I pleaded internally, neither of us oblivious to the fact that my stomach would soon start to swell with the piece of us we'd managed to create. His hand cupped the place where my bump would grow as he lowered himself between my legs.

"Absolutely beautiful," he whispered, and I silently prayed he would always believe that was true.

WHEN WE FINISHED, we lay together, both breathing heavily, soaked in cool sweat and staring up at the dingy ceiling of my bedroom. He twisted a finger through a wisp of my hair, and I thought of how much I loved these moments.

Why did he ever have to leave? Why couldn't he stay with me all the time? I knew my apartment was a farther drive for him to work than he'd like, but I'd said over and over that I'd move in with him if he wanted me to. He thought we were moving too fast, but this baby had sped things up, no matter the original plan. The ring he chose, the one I kept in my top dresser drawer had sped things up. Why was he still keeping one foot on the brakes? I believed it had to be a commitment issue, which explained why he was nearing forty-five and still single.

"What are you thinking about?" he asked, pulling me out of my thoughts. I turned my head to look at him.

"Nothing, really," I lied.

"You're lying." He called me on it.

My smile was small. "Just thinking about being with you. I wish it could be like this all the time."

47

His gaze became distant, like it so often did. He looked back up toward the ceiling. "I know. I do, too." His jaw was tight as he said it. I could've easily called him out on his lie, too.

"Am I doing something to scare you off?"

He propped up on one elbow and stared at me like I was being ridiculous. "Of course not, Alaina. Why would you ask me that?"

"Every time I bring up moving in together, you shut down."

"I've told you, your apartment is too far from my work."

I placed a hand on his chest. "And I've told *you,* I can do my job from anywhere. Let me move in with you. Let's get a place together somewhere different. Just give me a big window somewhere in the house, and I'll be satisfied. I just want you..."

He rubbed a hand over his scalp. "It's just not good timing right now. Work is too busy for me to think about moving, and my house is a total bachelor pad."

"I don't mind—"

"I said no, Alaina, okay?" His tone was harsh, and I knew the conversation was nearing its end. This was our stopping point. Our brick wall. I had no idea why I pushed him. No idea why I kept pushing him when it never ended anywhere different. This was where we always ended up. "I gave you a ring, didn't I? I said I would marry you. I will take care of you. Is that not enough?"

"Do you love me?" I asked, and sudden, betraying tears pooled in my eyes.

His jaw dropped, his eyes narrowing at me. "Of course I love you, Alaina. I wouldn't be here if I didn't."

There was a truth in his tone, real and palpable, and I knew he meant it. Still, it troubled me that he refused to take the next obvious step. "When, then? When will you move in with me? After we're married?"

"We won't wait that long," he promised, obviously thinking that would make me feel better.

"*That* long? How long are you planning to wait to marry me? The baby will be here in just a few short months."

"Seven months," he said quickly. "We still have seven months."

"They'll fly by."

"Enough, Alaina. This is all...it's a lot, okay? It's a lot, and it's overwhelming—"

I pushed up from the bed, grabbing my dress and tossing it over my head. "*You're* overwhelmed? Well, I'm incredibly sorry to have caused you any stress, Lucas. I can't imagine how that feels because I just live my life here in Happyville without a care in the world."

He stood up, pulling on his pants from the floor. His shoulders were tense, and I knew he was mad. I did that. Despite my usual efforts to keep him happy—I knew how much his work stressed him out—the baby had put a timer on what we had. A countdown. No longer could we continue to take a leisurely stroll through our relationship; I couldn't keep letting him stop in for an hour or two and then disappear from my life for days or weeks on end. I knew his life was busy—I wasn't needy and would never pretend to be—but I did need this. If he was going to be in this child's life, I needed him to step up before it arrived.

"I know that's not true, okay? I know you're just as stressed as I am, but you have to give me time. You know how I work. I push people away and I need my space, I just—"

"Take your space," I said, handing him his shirt with force. "Take all the space you need. But when you come back, I need you to know what you want from me. If I'm just a booty call you happened to knock up—"

"You know that's not it!" He reached for me, but I stepped back, rage boiling in my belly as I'd never felt it before.

"I know you've told me it's not, but I know how you're making me feel right now, too. We don't have long. I will do this on my own if I have to, but what I won't do, is do it with you having one foot out the door. You're either in our lives or you're out, Lucas. You have to decide, and you have to decide quickly. I can't take much more of this."

He pulled his shirt over his head, his expression stony. "You know that I love you."

"But do you love *us*?" I gestured toward my belly. "Do you love me enough to want all that comes with this?"

"I gave you a ring. I'm not sure what else you want from me." His dark brows drew down in frustration.

"I want it all, Lucas. And anything less than that couldn't possibly be enough." With that, I walked past him, fighting back tears as I pulled open the door. "You should go. I have a project due, and I need to get back to work."

I wanted him to fight, to argue, to say there was no way he would leave like this and pull me into his arms to let me know I was all he'd ever want or need.

Instead, he sighed, then left without a word or second glance.

CHAPTER TEN

NAOMI

When he arrived home, I knew it was going to be a rough afternoon. Already, he was groaning and angry, his movements tense and tight as he moved through the house. The birthday cake Becca helped me make was cooling on the counter as I ran the needle and thread through her pink sweater, attaching the tutu to its hem.

He came into the room before I turned around, hoping to alleviate his bad mood with a smile and chocolate. I ignored his anger.

"Welcome home." I held up the wings in a sort-of salute. "You'll never guess what your daughter wants to be for Halloween this year."

He laughed, but it was dismissive, and I wasn't sure if he was really listening to me. He headed to the counter and grabbed a glass, filling it with water and took a drink. "Nice," he said, not really responding to what I'd said.

I refused to ask how his day was, even though it felt like I should. I wouldn't do it. I didn't want to know. It was my birthday, and he was supposed to drop it at the door and celebrate with us. That was his promise this morning.

I stood, laying the costume on the table and walking to him. I rubbed a hand across his back. "We made a chocolate cake. Becca got to lick the bowl."

He rolled his eyes, his brows knitted in frustration when he turned to face me. "You know I hate it when you let her do that."

"I know," I said, keeping the smile planted on my face. "But she loves it." I waited, but he didn't smile back. "I only let her have a little bit." It wasn't true, but it didn't matter. I needed him to smile.

He finished the rest of his glass of water and set it in the sink. "What would you like for dinner, my love?" I swear sometimes I got whiplash from how quickly his mood changed, but still, there was a chill to his tone.

"I was thinking we could go out. That way no one has to cook or deal with dishes. What do you think? Jonathan's?"

"Sounds delicious." He kissed my lips quickly, not allowing me to savor him, and walked away. "I'm going to shower before we head out."

I nodded, letting him get midway down the hall before I headed back to the table to finish sewing.

I was running the last thread through the fabric of her costume when I heard the water kick on upstairs. I put the sweater down, sticking the costume in the bag and the bag on top of the fridge, then headed down the hall. Becca was asleep in her room, but she should've been waking up within the hour.

In the middle of the hallway, I turned and headed up the stairs toward the bedrooms. I walked through our bedroom, lifting his scrubs from the floor and tossing them into the hamper. The water shut off as I opened the door, suffocated by the steam that smacked me in the face. My skin was suddenly dewy.

He opened the glass door of the shower, jumping back when he realized I was standing there. He grabbed a black bath towel from the rack.

"What the hell?"

"I thought I could join you…" I whispered, running a finger along the side of the door.

He sighed, rubbing the towel through his wet hair. "I'm already getting out, Naomi."

"Well, God, I didn't realize it was such a chore." I was half joking, but he didn't seem to care.

"It's not a chore, but…just not right now, okay? Becca will be up soon, and you should start getting ready if we want to get a table."

"We have time if you want to…" I stepped forward, rubbing a hand over his wet torso. "It's my birthday, after all."

He sighed again. "I had a shit day at work, Nae." I hated it when he called me that, my mother's signature nickname for me, too. Like I was a barnyard animal. "I just need a minute, okay?"

Where had the man I knew this morning gone? "Anything you want to talk about?"

"I'd just as soon not. I just need some time to get it out of my head."

I stepped back. "Okay. Fair enough. I'll be downstairs icing the cake."

He ran the towel over the back of his neck. Before I got to the door, I looked back at him. "Oh, I meant to ask, do you want to be Winnie or Tigger? Becca wants us to dress up with her, and I'm going to grab some fabric while I'm out tomorrow."

He shook his head, wrapping the towel around his waist. "You know...just do whatever you want. I probably won't be able to do it anyway. I'll end up working."

"Well, we can go a different day if you have to work. I just plan to take her to my parents' or—"

"That's your thing, Nae, not mine. I don't want to dress up."

"It's not *my* thing. It's *our daughter's* thing. Don't you want to be a part of her childhood? These are the memories, Lucas. Right here. These are the things she'll remember, and if you aren't a part of them, she'll always know that and wonder why."

He groaned, patting his thigh. "Oh, great. Here we go. I haven't been home a half hour, and already you're in on me."

"In on you?"

"You always do this, Naomi. According to you, I'm never doing enough. Not making enough money, not present enough of the time, not nice enough when I am home, not firm enough with Becca, not playful enough with her, not enough. Not ever. When are you going to realize I'm not you? Try as I might, I'm never going to be you."

I blinked, surprised when my eyes began stinging with

tears. "I...I never asked you to be me, Lucas. You know how much being a parent means to me. You know how badly I want to give Becca what I never had."

"Yeah, I know," he huffed. "Because life as *Naomi freakin' Roberts* was just so terrible. All the money in the world while some of us were barely scraping by—"

"Money isn't love, Lucas." This was a fight we'd had before...so many times. He blamed me for growing up privileged and wealthy—despite the fact that my parents were never around—because he grew up poor, with an addict for a mother. "Money doesn't buy happiness. We've discussed this."

"Yes. Yes, we've discussed it, alright. 'Til I'm blue in the face, but that doesn't change the facts. You may not have always felt loved, Nae, but you were always safe. You were always protected. That's all I want to give Becca—"

"She'll always be safe, though. You don't have to fight so hard for that." I reached for his arm, but he pulled away, grabbing boxers from his dresser drawer and throwing them on.

"Yeah, because your family provides for us. But I don't want that, don't you understand? I want to provide for my daughter, my family. Do you have any idea how embarrassing it is that your family's money is still paying off my student loans because I don't make enough to afford the life we live?" He pulled a T-shirt over his head angrily.

"We have more money than we could ever need. Being a surgeon was what you wanted, Lucas, but you can't fault me for giving Becca everything she's entitled to. What would you rather me do? Pretend we don't have access to money? Pretend to live within the means you provide us with?"

"The means I provide us with are a hell of a lot more than I had as a child."

"So our child should do without?"

"You mean like I did?"

"You've said yourself you hated your childhood—"

"I did, Naomi!" He slammed a fist on the dresser. After he'd pulled on pants, he sank onto the edge of the bed, pulling on tennis shoes. "That's exactly the point. And I want to be the reason we aren't in a similar situation. I want it to be me."

"Well, I guess you married the wrong woman, then. You knew I came from money when we dated, when you asked me to marry you. If my finances are such a burden to you, by all means, leave now. Because I can't continue to apologize for having more than you did. I'm sorry, but I can't." I folded my arms across my chest, feeling hurt and angry. I was tired of having the same fight over and over. I was tired of feeling guilty because he wasn't satisfied with the income he was making compared to the enormous debt he was in when we met. I was tired of apologizing for giving Becca more than he had as a child.

He stared at me, shocked by my outburst. It was rare I stood up to him, but apparently forty was bringing out a whole new side of me. I inhaled sharply, my chest rising and falling.

"Fine," he said. "Maybe you're right. Maybe this whole thing was a mistake."

I stayed silent, suddenly unable to find the words to

say anything in response. He couldn't be serious. What had happened at work to put him in this bad of a mood?

"I'm going to go back to the hospital for the night. I can't...I can't be here."

"Lucas, wait..." It was my birthday, I wanted to remind him. Instead, he continued to walk, and I made no further attempt to stop him. My husband's shadow disappeared down the hall, and I listened to his footsteps traveling down the stairs and out the front door. When it slammed, I let out a heavy sob just as Becca's voice carried down the hall.

"Mom?"

CHAPTER ELEVEN

CLARA

When I walked into the locker room, Luke was already there, his hair messy with sleep, and he had a mug of coffee in his hand.

"I thought you weren't in this morning?" I asked, looking at my watch. He wasn't scheduled for surgery for a few hours, but I wouldn't tell him I knew that down to the minute.

He shook his head, taking a sip of the coffee and releasing a loud breath. "I came in late last night and crashed in the on-call room."

I looked over at the few other doctors around the room, surprised he'd admit that so openly. It was generally frowned upon to use the on-call rooms unless you were actually on call. "Did you get called in for a surgery?"

He stood and moved toward me as I hung my purse and jacket in my locker. "Nah, long story. Naomi and I got into it, and I just needed to get out of there. I was hoping to get a surgery to take my mind off it, but that didn't happen."

"Why didn't you call me?" I asked, lowering my voice even more. "You know you could've come over. My bed is much more comfortable than the on-call bed. You know that."

He tugged at a piece of my hair. "I know. I didn't want to bother you. It was late."

"Luke," I said, huffing out a breath. "You're always welcome at my house. It's why you have a key. Even if I'm not home, if you need somewhere to go, you go." I stared at him until he met my eye, but he finally did. "Deal?"

"Deal."

I wanted to kiss him, but I resisted the urge. "Do you want to come by tonight? Let things cool down at home?"

He pressed his lips together. "I work late."

"So? Come by when you get done. I'll be there."

He nodded, his expression filling with warmth. "Are you sure you want me there?"

"I *always* want you there," I said, and it was the truth. He smiled.

"Okay, thanks. I'll come by."

With that, he cupped my jaw and rubbed a thumb across my cheek quickly, his touch warm on my skin. He pulled his hand away as quickly as he placed it there and headed from the room. I grabbed my scrubs, my body pulsing with energy and adrenaline. *Oh, what that man does to me...*

———

I HEARD him coming through the front door, and though the apartment had been dark for hours, I was far from asleep. I'd been waiting anxiously like I was a teenager preparing for my first sleepover with a boy. It was always like that with Luke. Twelve years in, and every moment with him felt like the first time.

I listened as his footsteps carried across the apartment, hearing him easing himself into the bedroom. I sat up with a light, easy smile, pretending he'd woken me.

"What time is it?" I asked, as if I hadn't been staring at the clock for the past hour, counting down until he was there… And half wondering if he would be.

"Just past eleven," he whispered, pulling his scrubs off and tossing them to the floor. He opened the bathroom door and walked in, stark naked. I couldn't stop my eyes from traveling down the length of his body and back up again. He turned on the walk-in shower and looked himself over in the mirror. He was always doing that—checking himself out like he was God's gift to women. It made me feel guilty for doing the same. At least one of us should have their head on straight about his beauty…and it wasn't going to be him. It was one of the reasons we butted heads when I first started working.

He glanced over at me, obviously appreciating my stares, and his brows shot up. He grinned. "Wanna join me?"

I climbed from the bed without much coaxing, trying to hide the growing smile on my lips. "How was work?"

"I don't want to think about that right now," he said, shaking his head as he lifted the silk nightgown over mine. His eyes trailed down my body. There was a time when I was so embarrassed and self-conscious about the way I looked, sagging here and there, wrinkles where they weren't before, but with Luke, I was so comfortable now that I didn't care. He knew every inch of me. He knew where I was ticklish and where my body dimpled. He knew the ways I like to be touched.

He pulled my hand, dragging me into the shower and directly under the spraying water with him, oblivious to anything else. We kissed in the shower like two teenagers kissing in the rain. It was fearless, passionate, and carefree in a way I'd never been loved by anyone but him.

He cupped my neck, his long fingers wrapped in my hair as he sank further into my kiss. Kissing him was like breathing—so easy and instinctual I wanted to do very little else when I was with him. He ran his lips across my jawline, and I let out a moan. I'd never felt this good—not with anyone else, not even close.

"I love you," I whispered, my body hot with desire as the steam billowed around us.

"I love you, too," he said, his hands moving to explore my body. I could lose myself with him. Sometimes, I think I already had. Very little else mattered to me when he was around. For so long, my friends and parents had questioned why I stayed with someone who refused to commit in a serious way, but the fact was, I didn't need commitment when I had Luke. It sounded crazy, believe me I know, but being with him was the easiest thing in the world. However I could have him, that was how I would. I followed his timetable. When you were my age, that was what you did. So many men were afraid to settle down. They were set in their ways, and there was very little you could do to bring them out of it. With Luke, he bent me to my breaking point but knew just when to give. It was intoxicating. His love made me feel alive, and wasn't that worth a little risk?

"Where's your head?" he asked, pulling away from me with concern, and I realized I'd been thinking so much I'd stopped reacting to what he was doing.

I shook my head, rubbing my eyes. "Sorry," I said. "I'm just...nothing. Still half asleep, I guess." I grabbed at his face, trying to continue what I interrupted, but his hands left my body and I knew he didn't believe me. He knew me too well.

"Something's bothering you." He seemed almost hesitant to ask.

"I...I just hate that you stayed at the hospital and didn't come here last night," I said, grimacing. I really, really didn't want to fight.

"I know I should've come here, but I just hate showing up unannounced, and I didn't want to call you and wake you up."

"You're always welcome here, Luke. You know this place is as much yours as it is mine. We picked out everything here, including the actual apartment, together. Why do you still walk on eggshells about it?"

"I just want to be respectful," he said, and I saw a muscle in his jaw twinge.

"I know that, but you don't have to be. That's the whole point. If I had it up to me, you'd live here with me, or I with you. You mean so much to me, Luke. Don't you know that?"

"I do," he conceded. "Of course, I do." His hand slipped around mine, our fingers lacing together as he stared at me.

"So, you'll come to me next time? Instead of staying at the hospital?"

"Who's to say there'll be a *next time*?" He was avoiding the question, as usual.

"There's always a next time," I said. We both knew it was true. His sister was difficult to live with, at best, and the two seemed to fight more often than not. I didn't understand how someone in her predicament could be so ungrateful for all Luke had done for her. He was a better person than I was.

He sucked in a sharp breath. "Fine, next time I'll come here. I promise."

I nodded, accepting the small victory, but knowing it wasn't what I truly wanted to hear. "You know this place is yours, too…whenever you need it."

He kissed me gently, but there was a coldness there that wasn't present before. "I know."

Why couldn't he need it now? Why couldn't he want it now? Was my place not good enough for him? He chose it. I picked this apartment instead of the one I preferred, the one closer to downtown and work, because he had such strong opinions about that particular one. "I—I mean, you can stay here any time, permanently even." My gaze drifted to the floor as I spoke, the words coming out too fast. "Or…you know, I could stay with you some. Maybe having some help with Naomi and Becca would make things easier for you. Relieve some stress…"

His stance was stiff as he looked me over and, suddenly, I wasn't feeling as confident in the way I appeared to him. I crossed an arm over my naked stomach, drawing his eyes back up to me. "You don't have to—"

"I've actually been thinking a lot—" We spoke at the same time then stopped, and he laughed, rubbing a hand across the back of his neck.

"Go ahead," I said.

"I've actually been thinking a lot about that. About... you know, moving in with each other."

My heart flipped in my chest. *Is he serious?* If this was a joke, it was incredibly cruel. "You have?"

His eyes brightened, the tension leaving his shoulders in an instant as heat rose in my chest. "Yeah," he said. "I think it's something we should really consider. I mean, not right now, of course. I'll have to get Naomi settled somewhere new, somewhere close by, so I can keep an eye on her and still help with Bec when needed, but it's time that I moved on with my own life, right?"

I touched his chest, my heart fluttering as I stared into his dark eyes. It felt like my chest could burst with joy. "Yes, you deserve it, Luke. Oh, you really do." I leaned into him, hugging his wet torso. It took an extra second for his arms to fold around me, his cheek resting against my scalp. He took a deep, thoughtful breath, our bodies moving together as we stood there, just existing together for the longest time.

I'd never been so happy, but I couldn't help wondering if he felt the same. Based on his silence the rest of the night, I didn't think so.

CHAPTER TWELVE

ALAINA

Knock, knock, knock. I felt the thumps rather than heard them and pulled off my headphones, staring at the clock. *He's early.* I grabbed the envelope of cash on the entertainment center and crossed the room, shoving the paintbrush into the pocket of my apron. I swung open the door and gaped at him—the wrong him.

"What are you doing here?"

"Can I come in?" Lucas asked, eyeing the envelope. "Expecting someone else?"

I nodded. "Mr. Andino." My landlord. "It's the first."

He stepped across the threshold and into my living room. "If you pay with a check, it helps keep things straight and you have proof it was paid."

"I prefer cash," I said stiffly. It was just like Lucas to correct such a menial task. His way was always the best. Truth was, Mr. Andino was the best landlord I'd ever had. If he requested payments in cash, it was no problem for me. I'd never be able to tell Lucas that—he'd surely pick apart my landlord's motives for needing all cash payments, motives I cared nothing about. We were all just trying to get by.

His shoulders rose and fell with a heavy, weighted breath. "I'm sorry about the way I handled things the other day."

I glanced down at my paint-stained fingertips and picked at the paint underneath my fingernails, refusing to meet his eye. *I won't give in this time.* I wouldn't. "Okay."

"Are you, er, I mean, are we...okay?"

My vision narrowed at him, my arms tossed down at my sides. "Do you have an answer for me?"

His jaw locked, and I caught the tiniest hint of a smile, my stomach turning to stone in an instant. "I...look, I want to make it up to you."

"That's not an answer, Lucas." I crossed my arms as I watched him. I could nearly see the wheels turning in his head as he tried to think his way out of the mess he'd made, but I wouldn't let him. "Why did you even come here?"

"I wanted to make it up to you," he said, still not telling me what I wanted to hear. I stared at him, waiting. "I thought maybe we could go out of town for the night. I'm off today and tomorrow, so we could go for a hike up at Rock Island, maybe? You could bring your supplies and paint the sunset."

My heart fluttered at the idea, though I struggled to maintain my composure. "Why would we do that?"

He stepped toward me, and there was a pull from somewhere deep inside my stomach. I wanted to hate him, but I couldn't. I wanted to resist him, but I wouldn't. "Because I feel bad for what happened. I'd had a rough day at work, but I shouldn't have taken it out on you. I'm allowed to have an off-day, right?" His tone was light, but I knew what he was doing. He wanted me to admit I was wrong for snapping like I had, that this was all somehow my fault.

"You have to decide if you want this...all of this. Me. This baby. You have to decide, Lucas. I can't make the decision for you, and I can't keep going without knowing what you—"

"I want the baby," he said, reaching for my arms. I didn't stop him as his thumbs caressed my skin. I was nearly crying at the sentence. "I want all of it—you, our family. I want to be with you, Alaina. You know that. You shouldn't have to question it, and I'm sorry I made you. I gave you a ring—" He lifted my hand, looking for it, then glanced at me.

"I don't wear it when I paint." My expression was empty, hoping he'd believe that was the only reason. I hadn't worn it since he left, though it had taunted me from its hiding place in my drawer.

He pressed his lips to the place where it should go. "I gave you a ring because I wanted to be with you. I wouldn't have done it otherwise. And...I do want us to live together, but I want to do it right. I want to buy you a nice house, not coop you and the baby up in my tiny apartment or your tiny apartment. I wanted it to be a surprise, but that's what I'm working on. Getting us a new place...together. I just couldn't keep it a secret any longer."

I smiled, though it was small and forced. I couldn't be sure he was telling the truth, couldn't be sure he wasn't trying to charm me as usual. It was so easy for him to charm everyone, it could be hard to tell. He watched me carefully, his eyes darting back and forth between mine.

"Well, thank you, I guess," I said finally. "Though I'd love to be part of the process."

He nodded. "Then part of the process you shall be." He reached for my waist, and I didn't stop him, not as his fingers snaked across my hips, tickling my back until they came to meet in the center. His lips were just inches from mine. "So what do you say? Go away with me?"

"To Rock Island?"

He rubbed his nose against mine. "It's beautiful there. Like you."

I felt my face flush, to my own detriment, and I knew he had me. There was nothing I could do to stop it. "Okay."

AN HOUR LATER, we were in the car on the way to the getaway he had planned. The car was loaded up with my painting supplies and a bag of clothes and toiletries. Lucas seemed cool and collected, riding with the top down, his hand in mine on the center console. We whipped around a curve and he grinned, always driving too fast for my taste.

"Can't you just imagine the two of us? Traveling the world? No worries, no pressure, no stress?"

I tensed instantly at his words. "The two of us?"

He darted his gaze my way, his face falling. "The three of us, of course, but for now, two is nice, isn't it?"

I kept my lips pressed together because I was not sure

if it was a true slip or if he'd meant to leave the baby out of the equation. Either way, I wasn't sure which was worse, forgetting your child or willfully choosing to ignore their existence.

I pulled my hand from his and slid it across my belly, and he moved his hand to the steering wheel. Just like that, the air had shifted. Things were different between us. The baby had done that. Lucas had done that.

Problem was, I didn't know if things would ever be the same.

I didn't know if I wanted them to be.

When we arrived at the cabin, we'd ridden most of the way in silence. He seemed to be either blissfully unaware of the mood shift or perhaps hoping that I'd forgotten it happened.

Before I unloaded my bag, I grabbed the canvas and paint supplies and headed to the edge of the cliff behind the cabin he'd rented. It was beautiful there; he was right. The sun was setting just over the horizon, splashing the sky with a beautiful display of oranges, pinks, and reds. It would look breathtaking in paint, but I wasn't sure I wanted to capture this feeling forever. If it didn't sell, whenever I looked at it, I would remember this moment. The thickness of my strokes, the heavy paint I'd apply would always be indicative of the anger swelling in my chest right then.

Yet still, I painted. I propped up the easel and set the canvas on it, pulling out my oil paints and my apron. Lucas didn't follow me, and I realized he must not have been as oblivious as I thought. He knew my paints calmed me down, and he knew I needed the space.

I splashed the first bit of paint on the canvas, moving my brush to-and-fro to create the place where the yellow of the sky met the green of the earth.

I was lost in my painting, my worries seeming to fade away when I felt hands go around my waist, sliding around to cup my belly. He surrounded me with his body, his face resting near my ear. "Just wait until the little guy is big enough to bring out here and go fishing with his old man."

I pressed my lips together, rejecting the smile that tried to grow on my lips. "Or little girl."

"Or little girl," he conceded, stepping back and attempting to spin me around. I obliged, though I was right in the middle of a critical stroke in my work. If it dried for too long, it wouldn't work as I'd planned.

"I'm sorry, Lainie. Honestly. I'm a screw-up, okay? I'm really trying here, but...I'm going to mess up occasionally. It's not because I don't care, but it's truly just that I never had someone show me the right way to be a dad. Hell, I didn't even have someone to show me the wrong way."

"It's no excuse, Lucas. You can't tell me you've never seen a good dad in your life. I know you didn't have one, but that's not going to be your get-out-of-jail-free card every time you do the wrong thing here. I won't allow you to use that and hurt me or hurt our child." I was shaking with adrenaline. It was what had been swimming in my head for so long. "You have to decide if you want to do this. If you're all in. Because if you're not, I get it. I won't force you. I won't ask anything of you. But you have to decide now because I can't be on this roller coaster any longer."

He swept me in his arms, cradling me in a hug, and I hated the tears that welled in my eyes. "I've already decided, I told you that. I love you. I want to be with you. I want to raise our baby. You're just going to have to whip me into shape." He laughed, his breath hot on my ear.

"I can do that," I agreed, pulling away from him, but not too far.

He stared at me, his dark eyes meeting mine then traveling to my lips. He lowered his mouth to mine cautiously, his lips parting in what seemed like slow motion. I closed my eyes, wrapping one arm around his neck and pulling him to me. My body filled with warmth, with love, and with hope.

I wanted this to be right. I wanted to feel like he was telling the truth.

Somehow, despite it all, I couldn't shake the feeling that it wasn't. That, once again, I was being lied to. That I'd just strapped myself in for the latest ride on the roller coaster that was my life with Lucas. Why did I keep doing this to myself? Why did I let his dimples and dark eyes suck me in every time? I'd lost myself in him, and as much as that terrified me, I wouldn't have wanted it any other way.

CHAPTER THIRTEEN

NAOMI

When Lucas returned from his trip Thursday evening, I was at the door, already dressed and ready to go. I was sure he'd forgotten our plans the moment he saw me. The smile fell from his face and he raised his sunglasses from his eyes.

"Everything okay?" he asked, stopping in his tracks.

I swallowed. It was the first we'd spoken in person since our fight, and I wasn't sure where we stood. What I did know was that we didn't have time to worry about it.

"You've forgotten," I said, forcing out a breath. "We're supposed to be meeting my parents for dinner."

"Shoot," he said, glancing at his watch. "No, I hadn't forgotten. Not entirely. Give me just a few minutes to clean up, and I'll be ready."

"We have twenty-six at most, or we'll be late," I reminded him.

"That's sixteen more than I need," he promised, giving me a lopsided grin and hurrying past me, pressing a hand to my forearm as he did.

I paced the living room, smiling at Becca as she entered the room. "Are you ready to go see Grandma and Grandpa, sweetheart?" I looked her over, checking for crumbs or stains and dusting her off to be sure I wasn't missing any. I wouldn't dream of bringing her to my parents in any state other than perfect.

I heard the water shut off upstairs and, within minutes, Lucas was rushing down the stairs, dressed in his best jeans and a blue button-down shirt, his hair slicked back with gel.

"Ready?" He clapped his hands together, looking us over then scooping Becca from my arms and kissing her cheek before kissing mine. "Wow, my girls are beautiful." He smelled of spearmint mouthwash and bergamot cologne.

"Thank you, and thank you for hurrying."

"I'm sorry I was late. Traffic was a little worse than I expected."

"And you forgot?"

His lips seemed to be teetering between a grin and a frown. "And I forgot." His grip tightened on my hip as I grabbed my purse, Becca's bag, and the keys.

"How was your trip?" I asked as I slid the key into the lock, and he stood beside me, waiting.

"Boring as usual. Just another conference. How did things go here?" He bounced Becca in his arms. "Did you keep your mama in line?"

"Of course I did!"

She squealed with joy, and I smiled, shaking my head. "Everything was fine here."

I felt my phone buzz in my pocket as a text came

through, and though I knew who it was, I didn't dare check it. Not in front of Lucas. I couldn't. Last night was a moment of weakness. I shouldn't have texted him. Shouldn't have invited him over again. I'd been so strong since the first time.

Last night was a mistake.

Lucas could never know.

We walked toward the car, and he buckled Becca in before holding out his hand for the keys. I tossed them over and climbed into my seat, waiting for him to drive.

I should've been worried, should've been nervous he'd find out what I'd done. *Twice.* But I couldn't be. Not right then. I could only focus on one crisis at a time and, currently, that crisis was my parents.

"OH, NAOMI, YOU LOOK MARVELOUS, DARLING," Mom said, wrapping me in a hug with a stiff kiss on the cheek as we met at the door. She was dressed all in white, a loose top and capris to match her white heels and cool, blonde hair.

"So do you, Mom," I told her, stepping aside so she could reach for Becca.

"Hello, sweetheart." She took her from Lucas' arms and kissed her cheek, squeezing her tight and placing her down. Then, she went in for Lucas.

"And who's this handsome man?" She lit up, hugging him longer than either Becca or me. "I swear, you just get better looking every time I see you." She pulled away, one hand still around his neck. "Naomi still taking good care of you?"

"Yes, ma'am," he said, looking at me helplessly as his neck flamed scarlet. "Very good care of me."

She stepped back, releasing him. "Excellent. I'm so glad you all could make it. Our schedules do make it so hard sometimes. Your father's on the veranda, Nae."

We walked through the vast, airy entranceway, through the state-of-the-art kitchen, and out the back door into the oasis they called a backyard.

"Hey, Dad," I said as he stood up, laying his book on the table in front of him.

"Hello, sweetheart. Colette, you didn't tell me the kids had arrived." He hugged me, rubbing my back gently. "You look beautiful." He held out a hand for my husband to shake. "Are you keeping her out of trouble, Luke?"

Lucas nodded, accepting his handshake. "Doing my best, Walt. How was Italy?"

"Just beautiful," my mom answered. "It really is the best time of year to go right now. After most of the tourists have left and you can truly just settle in with the locals."

Dad nodded along dutifully. "She's right. You two will have to come with us next year. Oh, or, we're planning to go to Bora Bora next week. You should come then. They should come then, right, sweetheart?"

Mom gave a stiff grin. "Of course they should. They're always welcome. What do you think, kids?"

"If only I could get the time off work," Lucas said, rubbing the back of his neck. "One of our best surgeons just retired, so things are slammed right now."

My dad's face fell into a frown, though I knew he was expecting this answer. It was always the answer. When I was six, my father sold an award-winning script to a studio that hit it big. Since then, he had dabbled here and there in producing and writing, but they'd been traveling on his royalties all my life. Usually, I was left behind with a nanny, which seemed to be the way they enjoyed it. I could count the number of times, on one hand, I'd been able to go along. Now that I was with Lucas, and they knew our schedule wouldn't allow it, the invitations had begun to come more often.

"Well, another time then," he said with a sigh. "Now, how about some drinks? We brought some amazing wine back that you'll just have to try. Of course, we couldn't bring back all we would've liked to."

"Right, yeah. That sounds great," Lucas said, scooping Becca up as she began to run circles around the sharp edges of their glass coffee table. "Easy there."

"I'd love a glass, Dad," I said. "Please."

"Oh, you're in for a treat." He clapped his hands together and hurried back into the house, seeming more excited than he had in a long time. We followed close behind, and I kept an eye on Lucas who was struggling against Becca's attempts to get back on the floor.

"Do you want to go out and play in the yard?" he asked, but she shook her head.

"No, I want to stay with you."

"That's fine, sweetheart, but you know you aren't supposed to run inside the house, right? You'll fall and get hurt."

"I won't fall!"

I reached for her. "Becca, mind your father. We don't want you getting hurt."

She crossed her arms to pout, but was distracted by my parent's cat as it darted across the floor. Lucas set her down, letting her follow the cat and smiling at my mom who watched the interaction closely.

"Be careful, Bec," I warned. "No running."

She slowed her gait instantly. In the kitchen, Dad poured four glasses of wine and passed them out. "So, tell us, Luke, what have you been up to lately? Any interesting surgeries?"

Lucas seemed shy, though I knew it was a put-on. There was nothing he loved more than bragging about his latest surgery. "It's been a slow few weeks. We had a tumor that was growing teeth a few months ago, did I tell you—"

"Yeah," Dad interrupted, looking positively delighted, "you told me about that one. Disgusting. I tell you, I don't know how you do it, son. One look at blood, and I'm toast. Ask Colette." He pointed at my mom, who nodded, appearing unamused.

"It's true."

Lucas scratched the back of his neck. "It fascinates me, the way it all works, how resilient the body is."

"I'm just amazed at how *resilient* you two are," Mom cooed. "I tell you, I never thought anyone would get Naomi to settle down, and I was just telling Walter the other night I actually believe you two are going to see it through." She patted Lucas' chest. "I had my doubts at first, but you both seem so happy."

"Thanks, Mom," I said bitterly, taking a sip of my wine to keep myself from saying much more.

"Oh, you know what I mean, darling. You were never

the type who wanted to settle down. Always roaming and wandering."

"Getting life experience, mhm," I said, teasing her, though she didn't hear the sarcasm.

"You can get life experience with someone by your side, can't you Luke? It wasn't practical for a woman Naomi's age to be so...free."

I rolled my eyes, looking away, and Lucas seemed to sense the tension. "Well, lucky for me, I convinced her to settle down, Colette. I don't know what I'd do without her."

I looked over at him, surprised by his words. It had been so long since I'd heard anything remotely close to that, especially in the middle of a fight that had only fallen to a simmer, not completely lost its heat.

Did he mean it?

He met my eye again, his jaw tight, and he nodded slightly, just enough for me to catch it. My lips upturned. It was a show for my parents. We were a united front with them, and until we left, the fight had been forgotten. Here, nothing else mattered.

My mother heaved a sigh, and when I followed the sound with my gaze, I realized she was watching our interaction carefully. "Look at them, Walt," she said, hands clutched together in front of her chest. "Just like no one else is in the room."

I smiled sadly but looked away. Truth was, Lucas and I both knew we were only like this *because* others were in the room.

When we were alone, it was never so good.

CHAPTER FOURTEEN

CLARA

I scrolled through the patient's file on my way down the hall, concerned about his liver enzymes, though everything else appeared to be normal. When I reached the nurses' station, I handed off the iPad to one of the nurses behind the desk. "Can you run a complete panel for the patient in two twelve? Page me as soon as they're in."

"Of course." She nodded, looking over the chart as I turned away.

"Excuse me?" I glanced to my left, where a young woman with olive skin and dark, shoulder-length hair was staring at me. "Are you a doctor?"

"I am." I looked her over quickly, though she appeared fine. "Is everything okay?"

"It's my sister. She's...she's in pain." She glanced behind her, down the hall.

"Take me to her," I said, though she was on the move before I had to give the go-ahead. We rushed down the hallway, stopping at the first door on our left, and she brought me in.

The girl in the bed was nearly identical to the one who'd come to find me, though she looked to be a few years younger. Her hands were pressed into the bed at her sides, a grimace on her face. I moved toward her bed, lifting the iPad from her monitor. "Hi, I'm Doctor DeVoss. You're...Siobhan?"

"Yes," she said, her voice strained. Like her sister, I detected a slight English accent. "Nice to...to meet you."

"Well, let's see what's causing you an issue, and then we'll decide that, hm?" I joked, scrolling through her chart. I glanced at the board on the wall. "Has the nurse been in since eleven?"

The older sister shook her head, biting her lip.

"And where are you hurting? At the incision site?"

The girl nodded quickly, rubbing her hand over her gown where the appendectomy scar was covered by gauze.

"Well, you're not quite ready for your next dose, but it's possible you're metabolizing your pain medication a bit too quickly and it's worn off early. I'd like to try a different type of pain medication, something similar to what you'd get over the counter to see if we can combat that pain a bit until we can safely get you something stronger. I'd just like to take a look first if that's okay?"

"Su-sure." She winced as I laid her bed back a bit more, and lifted her gown just enough that I could see the gauze. I pulled it back gently, looking over the incision. She sighed with relief as the pressure was taken off her wound. "That feels better."

I smiled. "If your medication was wearing off, sitting in that position may have been putting too much pressure on your wound. Let's keep you laid back for the rest of the day if we can. This all looks fine," I told her, placing the gauze back over the wound. "It looks like Dr. Martin was your surgeon?"

She nodded, looking at her sister with a wide, goading grin. The eldest girl's face flushed crimson, and she covered her mouth.

"What's funny?" I asked, pulling my gloves off as I adjusted her blanket and put in an order for her medication. I was thinking of Luke at the mention of his name, though I tried to avoid it.

Siobhan shook her head, looking back at me from the bed with a smug grin. "Is Dr. Martin married?"

My blood ran cold at the question. "No. No, he's not. Why do you ask?"

"*Stop*," the older sister begged, her face even darker red than before.

Siobhan wrinkled her nose at her sister, the pain apparently all but subsiding. "Told you." She turned her attention to me. "Emma thinks he's hot and he was totally flirting with her, but she said anyone who looks like that must be married."

My body tensed, and I took in the girl's appearance closely. She was young—half my age—and beautiful, there was no doubt. Her sleek, dark hair, even tied back in a messy ponytail, was to die for, while mine was thinning and frizzy from years of bleaching. Her skin was creamy smooth and wrinkle-free, and even here in the hospital where she'd no doubt been up all night, she was still wide-eyed and awake. I'd gotten eight hours and had been yawning all morning.

"He was, hm?" I tried to seem more casual than I felt.

"Well, he asked if I was from around here," she said, crossing one arm around herself. "Though I'm sure he was just being polite."

I started to agree, but Siobhan cut me off.

"He asked if you've tried that restaurant called The Pharmacy, and when you said no, he said you should go some time. He said *we*, as in you two, should go some time."

Emma narrowed her eyes at her sister, though she didn't argue. Surely Luke was just being polite. He wasn't hitting on a young patient's anxious family member, was he? There was no way. I'd never seen him be anything less than professional with patients.

"I made a complete fool of myself anyway," she said with a sigh.

"Oh, I'm sure you didn't..." I cocked my head to the side. I should've wanted her to, but I couldn't. She seemed too sweet to have ill will toward. She reminded me so much of my sweet baby cousins—the closest things I had to nieces or daughters.

"I did. When he said it, I said I'd love that, but my voice was so high and squeaky I nearly choked. It was mortifying. He didn't say anything else at all."

"I told you, he'll come back," Siobhan pointed out.

"No, he—"

"Actually," I spoke up, but immediately regretted it, "he will. He'll want to check on your sister once before the end of his shift. Dr. Martin is very nice. I'm sure he was just trying to make you feel comfortable."

Emma nodded, her expression visibly shifting from hopeful to embarrassed. "I'm sure you're right. God, Siobhan, you're so embarrassing." She cast her gaze back to me. "Thank you for...for taking care of my sister."

"It was my pleasure," I said, a small, forced smile on my face. "A nurse will be in shortly to administer your medication. If you have any issues, just push that button there near your head and someone will check on you."

"Thank you," Siobhan said, a winning grin on her face as she looked back at her sister. I rushed out of the room, struggling to breathe and maintain my composure all at once.

I wanted to believe it couldn't be true, but there was nothing in the girls' expressions that resembled a lie.

Was Lucas growing bored with me? Could he be considering cheating?

CHAPTER FIFTEEN

ALAINA

I ran the brush over the canvas, painting the pale peach color of my skin onto the aqua blue background. My brush twisted and twirled with every curve of my body. I traded brushes, dipping the next in black and tracing the outline of my breasts, my hips, my fingers, my legs. I traced around my jaw, drawing the place where my ears connected with my head, the bends of my fingers against my thighs, the line where my lips connected, separating just so in the middle.

I paid special attention to the areas I wanted him to notice most, the areas I wanted to be burned into his memory.

When I was finished, when my body was lined in detail, shaded, and painted onto the canvas, I stood back and admired the work. Six hours had passed with my music roaring in my ears, lulling me into a quiet place of serenity while I worked. It was my favorite place to be—inside my own head with no one around to bother me, no noises to distract me, so deep inside my own subconscious that the music itself had dulled to white noise.

I looked over my work, noticing the places where it could've been stronger, but my legs were beginning to shake and my mouth was dry. I pulled my apron over my head and laid it on the bed, walking down the hallway with one hand resting on my stomach. I was tired, and though I hadn't changed much physically yet, my stamina had changed dramatically. The long painting sprints I'd once enjoyed so much now took it out of me. I had to be more careful, but of the paintings I'd done in recent years, today's was the one I was most proud of.

If I'd done well enough, perhaps it would bring Lucas back to me. Perhaps he would realize how much he missed me. Since the pregnancy, our time together had become less and less, to the point that I rarely saw him at all anymore. He was pulling away from me, and if I didn't do something, if I didn't act quickly, I was going to lose him forever. While, at one point, I didn't think that scared me so much, I now knew differently. The trip had changed something in me. It made me realize how badly I needed him. I didn't want to do this alone. I didn't want to be a single mother, a starving artist trying to raise a child on my own. I wanted Lucas. And, more importantly, I wanted Lucas to want me.

I filled a glass with water and sipped it as I made my way back down the hall and toward the bedroom, resting against the bed as the paint began to lose its sheen, drying against the canvas.

When it was nearly dry and my water was gone, I set the glass down and lifted my phone from the top of the dresser, pausing the music I'd forgotten to when I removed my headphones.

Lately, whenever I glanced at my phone, there was a sickening feeling of hope that I'd have a new message or missed call from him, but as per usual, the screen was blank.

I swiped my thumb across the screen, opening the camera, and held it out to snap the picture. The bad lighting and low-quality camera didn't make for the best picture, but it was good enough. If he wanted to see the real thing, he could come over. I considered adding that to the message, but changed my mind. My art would speak for me.

I took a deep breath, wondering what his reaction would be. Would he rush over, shove open the door, and gather me in his arms while overcome with desire? Would we someday hang both of our portraits on the walls of our bedroom for our own private viewing? A girl could dream, I supposed.

I took a deep breath, my thumb hovering over the green arrow. Once I hit it, things were out of my hands.

The ball would be in his court.

Send.

CHAPTER SIXTEEN

NAOMI

Somewhere across the room, Lucas' phone buzzed. I opened my eyes slowly, hesitantly, with sleep blurring my vision. Most nights, he kept his phone on loud in case he got called into work. It was only on a very rare night that he silenced it. Still, we were both used to waking up at the slightest noise from it, signaling that someone needed his help. Signaling that, soon, I'd be on my own again.

"Who is it?" I asked, glancing over toward his side of the bed with a closed eye. I sat up. *Where is he?*

To my surprise, my husband was nowhere to be found. His screen lit up the ceiling with its reflection, and I threw the covers off my legs, scooting across the bed. I lifted the phone, pulling the charging cord from its port and glanced at the screen.

A?

The image on the screen was small, and I couldn't quite make it out, though my sleep-coated eyes were no help. I leaned forward, typing in his password—his birthday—and opened it. There were no messages from the saved number aside from the small picture in the inbox. I clicked on it, pulled it up, and gasped.

The picture was of a painting, badly lit, but beautiful nonetheless. The woman painted on the canvas was completely naked, with intricate detailing across every nook and cranny of her well-formed curves. I stared at it closer—she had short, raven hair and small facial features and one hand was placed against a flat stomach.

What is this?

It looked as though the painting was freshly done, still sitting on a canvas in a dimly lit room. Who had sent this? What did they want? Who was A?

I clicked on the contact and repeated the number in my head. It was local. Since when was Lucas interested in art?

My stomach was in a tight knot, everything in me screaming that something wasn't right here. I went back to the picture again, staring at it closer. The woman's eyes held mine, startlingly realistic in their rendering. There was seduction in her expression...so why had it been sent to my husband? A sickly feeling washed over me as I moved around the bed quickly, typing the number into my phone and then deleting the picture from his.

I hurried back around the bed as I heard him on the stairs below, headed my direction. I plugged his phone back in and placed it back on the nightstand, launching myself onto the bed and throwing the covers over me, my heart racing, as the door swung open.

He walked across the room, staring at me strangely. "Everything okay?"

"Mhm," I said, breathless. "Why?"

"I thought I heard you walking around from downstairs."

"I just..." *Needed to slow my heart.* "Had to pee. Where were you?"

He lifted his phone from the nightstand, and I held my breath, watching him closely. He eyed it for a moment, then laid it back down and sighed before climbing into bed. "I was thirsty. I went for water."

I rolled over, my heart still thudding so loudly I was sure he could hear it from just across the bed. My phone was still clutched in my hand, though I didn't dare move to put it up.

"Good night," he whispered, and I felt the bed moving as he rolled away from me. I sighed, my thoughts jumbling as I tried to piece together exactly what had happened. Perhaps Lucas had just been searching for a piece of art, but why the initial? Why did he have the 'A' saved without a full name? If it was someone random, why was the number saved at all?

A for art, maybe? It was a possibility, but it seemed far-fetched.

No. Something else was happening. I felt it in my bones and, though I wasn't sure I could put a name on it just yet, I knew it wasn't good. Could Lucas have been cheating on me? I'd never suspected him of being unfaithful before. His job kept him so busy, he'd never have the time. Was I wrong? I'd need to get to the bottom of this, and I was making it a priority to do so.

Whoever you are, A, I'm going to find out.

CHAPTER SEVENTEEN

CLARA

"I n you go," Luke whispered in my ear as I took a seat at the kitchen table. He pushed my chair in behind me before making his way around and sitting as well.

"Thank you." I lifted the bottle of wine and poured it into both our glasses.

"This looks delicious," he said, cutting out a slice of lasagna and placing it on my plate carefully before serving himself. "Did you make the—"

I stood up and hurried toward the stove, where my bread was likely burning. "Yes, I almost forgot." I opened the oven and grabbed the dish towel from the counter, pulling out the pan.

He followed me over, wrapping his arms around me as I worked to move the bread from the pan to a plate. I only prepared meals like this when Luke was around. Ordinarily, I preferred microwaved meals, and I'd never cook anything just to put it in another bowl to serve it. But with Luke, I wanted everything to be special. I wanted him to feel like he deserved the best, because he did.

He grabbed the last piece of bread lightly, lifting it to his lips and taking a bite.

"It's going to be hot," I warned, though he already had it in his mouth. He sucked in a breath, trying to cool it down as he chewed.

"I know, but I can't wait." When he swallowed, he put the bread down and spun me around to kiss my lips. "Would you still love me if I had garlic breath?"

I giggled. It was one of his games. Would you still love me if... "I'd still love you no matter what, you know that."

He pressed his lips to mine, his hands wrapping around my waist as he trailed kisses from my lips to my ear and down my neck. I gave in, closing my eyes and losing myself in his touch as I leaned back into the stove, pushing in one of the knobs accidentally. The gas began to pop, threatening to ignite a burner, and we jerked away, laughter exploding from my chest.

"Okay, come on, before dinner gets cold," I told him, lifting the plate from the counter and walking it toward the table.

"Dinner might just have to wait," he teased, patting my bottom as we sat down. He was in an exceptionally good mood that evening, and I had no idea why. I liked to think it was because of me, but I could never be sure.

"How was work today?" I asked, changing the subject. As much as I wanted to be with him, my stomach was growling. I needed to eat something.

"Same as usual," he said, tearing off a piece of bread and popping it into his mouth again. "How was your day? What did you do?"

"Cleaned up a bit, I've been driving myself crazy over

the shower, so I finally had a chance to clean it up and catch up on laundry."

He reached for my hand, running his fingers over my knuckles. "I missed you."

I lowered my brows at him. "What's gotten into you?" I teased, though he tensed at my words and I instantly regretted it.

"What do you mean?"

"You're in an awfully good mood."

He smirked. "I've just had a good day, that's all. And I'm glad to be ending it with you."

"How's Naomi?" I asked. I was usually careful not to bring her up, especially when he was in a good mood, but I had to ask. After our last conversation about her, if I wanted to push for him to move in with me, now was the chance.

"Naomi's Naomi. No change really." He shrugged then changed the subject. "Is this a new sauce?"

"Same as always," I said, running a fork over my lasagna before taking a bite. "I meant to tell you, I had a patient ask about you the other night. She said she thought you were flirting with her." I smiled, trying to show him I was joking, but I truly wanted answers.

"What patient?" he asked, looking at me as if the suggestion was absurd. Of course it was.

"Well, it was the sister of a patient, actually. Emma something."

"Well, that narrows it down," he said with a snort.

"Do you make a habit of flirting with a lot of Emmas?"

He frowned, laying down his fork. "I don't make a habit of flirting with anyone but you, and you know that.

Why would I need to? I've certainly got my hands full already."

I was shocked by his words. "Do you?"

He moved to lift up his fork but stopped. "What's that supposed to mean?"

I took a bite, chewing my food to allow myself time to think. "I just...I mean, it's not like I take up very much of your time, do I?"

"What are you saying, Clara?"

He leaned forward, and I recognized the look in his eyes. It was the same one I'd seen him give patients when he was listening to their concerns while really mentally checking out. He was finished with the conversation before it had even begun.

"I just mean that...well, we aren't all that serious, are we? I love you, of course, but it's not like we live together. We don't see each other outside of work more than once or twice a week most weeks."

"Our schedules are crazy. You know I see you as often as I can."

"I know that," I said, reaching for his hand. He turned his over to allow me to hold it. "I do. Of course, I do. But...if we lived together, if we were married, we'd see each other even more, without having to try. Mornings, evenings, days off. Don't you want that for us? Wouldn't it just be easier?"

He drew in one side of his mouth, glancing down. "It would be easier, sure. It would be a dream, Clara. But dreams don't always work out as they should. What if we move in together and realize we don't like each other as much as we thought? What if it doesn't work out?"

"Is that what you're afraid of? Sure, that would be terrible, Luke, but isn't it worse not knowing at all? Isn't it worse just imagining all that could go wrong instead of enjoying what could be right? Is that what you're doing? Hiding from the possibilities?"

"I'm not hiding," he said firmly. "I love you, and I love what we have. I just don't see why we have to complicate things."

"Complicate?" I pulled my hand away. "Is that what I am to you? A complication?"

"Clara, no, I didn't mean—"

I pushed away from the table, the roar of my chair against the linoleum interrupting him. "Are you ever going to want everything with me, Luke? Or is this all there is for us? Because if this is it—dinners and rare dates, coming over in the middle of the night for sex—then I need to know now."

"Don't make it seem like you're some..." He groaned. "Like I'm using you. I've been good to you, Clara. I take care of you. I love you as much as I can right now. I've got so much on my plate, and—"

"Is this all there is for us? This?" I repeated, fighting back bitter tears as they filled my eyes. "I just need a yes or a no."

He cocked his head to the side, staring at me strangely. "Things have always been so good with us. Why are you pushing for more now?"

"Because, Luke, I'm not getting any younger. So much of my life has been wasted on the wrong men and the wrong careers, and I'm finally figuring it all out. I've given you so many years of my life, and we're no closer to commitment than we were back then, are we?"

"I'm committed to you, Clara. What will it take to show you that? I love you. I'm in love with you. I tell you that every day."

I stood up and he did the same, though I wasn't trying to get past him, only closer to him. "I need you to do more than tell me. I need you to prove it. I need you to take the next step."

His face went ashen. "Marry you?"

"God. Is that such a scary thing?" I brushed a tear from my cheek. *Please say no. Please say you will.*

"I can't marry you, Clara."

I let out a noise somewhere between a sigh and a sob. "What do you mean you *can't*?"

His eyes darted between mine, his lips parting. "I…" He hung his head, breaking eye contact. "I should've told you sooner. I was just so afraid to lose you."

"Told me what, Luke? What are you talking about?" Ice-cold fear filled my intestines.

"I don't believe in marriage. As much as I love you, I'll never be able to marry you."

I sucked in a sob. "W-what? How could we have gone this long and that never came up?"

"Because I was a coward," he said, placing a hand on his forehead. "Because I never wanted to lose you or hurt you or break your heart. I didn't want to disappoint you— I don't."

I backed away from him. "I can't believe this."

He stepped toward me, reaching for my hands. "I don't want to fight—"

"I just need some space," I said, turning away from him and making my way around the table. "I'm sorry, I think you should go."

He took hold of my arm and spun me around, his eyes swimming with tears of his own. "I won't survive losing you. Tell me what I can do. Please, Clara. I'll do anything. Anything except that."

I shook my head. "I don't know if there's anything you can do. I want a husband, Luke. Maybe not today, but someday. You knew that. You've always known that. I want to build a life together. To live together."

"I'll do it," he blurted out. "I'll move in with you. Will that help? Will that prove how committed I am?"

I shook my head with disbelief. Could he truly mean it? "I don't want to force you..."

"You aren't. I swear you aren't. I've been holding back for so long because I knew you'd expect me to marry you. I never wanted to have this conversation, but I should've so long ago... Let's move in together."

I batted back tears of a new kind, my heart swelling with hope. "Are you sure?"

"I've never been more sure," he said, wrapping his arms around me. I didn't fight back, the food and fight forgotten as he scooped me up, pressing me against the wall in a tender kiss.

I ran my hands through his hair, my tears landing on his cheeks. "I love you, Lucas Martin."

"I love you, too, Clara. More than you'll ever know."

His heart thudded against mine as he kissed me again, then he pulled away. His eyes were lost and cold, a stunning contradiction to his words.

"Is everything okay?" I asked, staring at him as he lowered me to the ground.

He nodded, forcing a smile that didn't meet his eyes. "Everything's perfect." He swallowed, unable to meet my gaze as he ran a finger over his lips, a telltale sign he was lying about something, as he wiped away my kiss.

He kept hold of my hand with his opposite hand, though he seemed to have forgotten he had it.

He was lying to me. About something, maybe about everything. Either way, I had to learn the truth.

His phone rang, interrupting my thoughts, and he pulled it from his pocket. I noticed the name, or rather letter on the screen, though he tried to hide it from me. *A.*

Who is A?

"Hello?" He answered the phone, walking away from me, though I kept up with him, pretending to be oblivious to his sudden need for privacy. "What are you talking about? I didn't—" He spun back around, noticing my presence. "Hold on. Hold on, okay? I'll be there in a half hour." He nodded, then hung up the phone and stared at me.

"What was that about?"

"It was the hospital. I got called in for a surgery. Can I take a rain check?"

I swallowed. "Who's A?"

He shook his head. "What?"

"On your phone, it showed A."

"H," he corrected, "for the hospital. I've got to go." He was lying. I knew what I'd seen...didn't I?

"Will you come back after? I can save you some food."

"I'll just crash there," he said dismissively as he made

98

his way toward the door and stopped to slip on his shoes. "It'll be a late one. I'll see you tomorrow morning." He kissed my lips, brushing my hair from my eyes as he darted away. To my surprise, he looked the most relieved he'd looked all night, to be leaving me.

Again, he was lying, and it was obvious there was so much I didn't know.

Of course, the most pressing question continued to repeat in my head: *Who is A?*

CHAPTER EIGHTEEN

ALAINA

I could hear him panting through the phone as he rushed out the door. I wasn't sure if he was at work or at home, but he made no effort to stall. When I called, he came running. I heard his car door shut before he spoke again, his voice slightly muffled by the engine starting.

"Now," he said, his voice going quiet for a moment as the car switched to Bluetooth, "what are you talking about? What painting?"

"The painting I sent you the other night. Don't act like you didn't get it."

"I have no idea what you're talking about, Alaina. You had a painting sent to my house?" His voice was strained, and I could tell he was stressed. What was he so worried about? How would I have sent anything to his apartment when I didn't have the address?

"No. I texted you a picture of my latest painting, Lucas. You said you wanted one like the one I'd painted of you, only of me..." I trailed off. Had I sent it to the wrong number? It wasn't possible, but I put my phone on speaker and checked just to be safe. "I have it right here. It shows it was delivered."

"When did you send it?"

"Last night. It was late."

He sighed. "I never got any messages from you last night. Was there any text with it?"

"No...just the picture. I thought it spoke for itself."

He seemed a bit calmer when he spoke again. "You should be careful sending messages like that. When I'm at work, interns often check my phone and read me the messages aloud."

"I know that. You've told me I can't send anything too risqué, but this was just art for all anyone knows."

He grumbled. "Well, when do I get to see this art, then?"

"Come over and you can see it right now," I teased, relieved to hear his stress disappearing.

He laughed under his breath, and I could swear I heard his engine revving. "I'll be there in twenty minutes."

LIKE HE'D PROMISED, within twenty minutes, he was coming in the front door. I stood from the couch as soon as I saw him, his gaze raking over me, though I was a sheer disappointment in my yoga pants and baggy T-shirt with no makeup. The baby had my morning sickness acting up, and it was all I could do to get dressed at all—though Lucas may have preferred I didn't. He walked toward me, scooping me in his arms and pressing his lips to mine.

He tasted of garlic, and I pulled away. "Did I interrupt dinner?"

"Yeah, I'd just gotten home, sorry. Can you smell it on me?" He covered his mouth, his cheeks flaming red.

"My nose is extra sensitive these days. It's not bad... just a bit garlicy."

He smiled, but didn't offer to brush his teeth. We were still pressed together, though there was starting to be a small bump between us. "So, where's this painting?"

I took his hand, pulling away from him and sucking in garlic-free air. Together, we walked down the hallway and into the bedroom. I pulled the cover from the canvas and stepped back, watching as he took it in. His face was pink for an entirely different reason then, and he moved forward, his fingers tracing the lines of my body with precision. "This is beautiful, Lainie." I smiled softly, watching his hand move across the canvas, taking extra time around my more sensitive areas. "I definitely would've let you know if I received this." When he turned back to me, his brow raised. "Do you think you sent it to the wrong number?"

I pulled out my phone. "I'm positive I didn't. Look."

He took the phone in his hand, staring at the photo and then up at the top where his number was. He shook his head, pulling out his own phone and scrolling through his texts. When I moved around to see his screen, he shoved it in his pocket. "I must've had bad service or something and it never came through. I worked late last night."

I wasn't quite buying the excuse, though I had no true idea where he might've been or why he'd lie. Instead of arguing further, I grabbed hold of his collar and pulled him toward me. "Well, now that you're here in person, perhaps you'd like to inspect the subject up close."

He gave a crooked grin, stepping closer. When he pressed himself against me this time, I could feel his excitement against my leg. He pulled his shirt over his head, then mine, staring down at my naked form.

"Yes, you seem to have gotten a few things right," he told me, his hands moving to my hips as he removed my pants then shot back up to cradle my head in a kiss.

I reached for his pants, our lips still locked together as I unbuckled his belt and shimmied the pants to the floor. He eased us onto the bed, our naked forms intertwined, my heart thudding in my chest. I couldn't explain the way he made me feel—like I could explode from sheer joy. I loved him more than I could describe. He filled me with warmth and hope and desire like I had never known before.

He sucked in a breath and the smell of garlic hit me again. This time, I had to jerk away. "I'm sorry." I put a hand over my mouth and sat up. He lay beside me, seeming confused. "It's the garlic. Would you mind rinsing your mouth? My morning sickness has gotten bad lately."

"Sure," he said, somewhat hesitantly. He stood from the bed and sauntered away. I could tell I'd upset him, but I couldn't put myself through that torture. I stared down at the floor, trying to regain my composure as I heard him sifting through drawers, looking for the mouthwash.

When the nausea had passed and I heard the water running, I realized I was staring at his pants, the lump of his phone evident in his pocket. Acting quickly, I reached down and pulled the phone out. Though he didn't know it, I'd seen him type his phone's password in before, yet I'd never once snooped. It was his birthday, and I typed it in quickly, going straight to his messages. He was right, there was no message from me, as there was no message thread at all from me. I went to his contacts—did he even have my number saved?—and typed in my number, surprised to see my name pop up as only an initial: A.

I furrowed my brow as I heard the water shut off and he began to gargle with the mouthwash. I didn't have much time. I closed out of the contacts and went back to the green message icon, scrolling down through his recent conversations hurriedly.

Naomi:

Where are you?

At work. Need something?

No, I'll take care of it.

Ethan:

Thanks for covering this morning. I've got you next time.

No problem. Everything went fine. Patient's recovering.

Good.

C:

Are you still at work?

Yes. You here?

Yes. I'll find you.

M:

Are you coming over?

Be there later tonight.

K.

Except for very recent conversations, his message history was blank. Who were these people? Who was Naomi? Why were so many of us saved in his phone under initials? C? M? A? What was he hiding? I heard him spit and hurriedly placed his phone back in his pocket. As he reentered the room, I tried my best to put on a warm smile and pretend my head wasn't spinning. Was Lucas cheating on me?

He couldn't be...could he?

He walked toward me, lowering his face just inches from mine. "Better?" he asked.

His breath was, but now I felt like I could be sick for an entirely different reason. I nodded, barely able to look at him, but he didn't seem to care as he met my eyes once, then stood and reached for my head, pushing the top of it down until I was staring directly at his erect form. He pulled my mouth toward him without warning, and I opened on instinct. His head went back from up above me as I wrapped my lips around him, my mind elsewhere completely. I had to think of something, anything.

He groaned, both hands on the sides of my head now as he moved me with increasing rhythm. I'd had a friend once who installed a tracking app on her boyfriend's phone when she believed he was cheating. If I could get my hands on Lucas' phone again, I could do the same. To do that, though, I'd have to convince him to stay the night and fall asleep long enough for me to get it.

I looked up at him, his face filled with desire as he bit his lip. I placed both of my hands at his base, swallowing my vomit in my throat and pretending to enjoy it as much as he was.

He wouldn't be the only one lying this time.

WHEN WE WERE DONE, we fell back on my bed together, our bodies slick with sweat. Lucas was tired, already yawning as his head hit the pillow.

"I should probably head home," he whispered, one eye closed. His hand gripped my breast possessively.

I threw a leg over him. "I wish you'd stay."

He gave a lopsided grin. "Then your wish is my command." I ran a hand through his hair, playing with it gently as he began to doze off. I'd always believed his face was especially handsome in the moonlight, moody and dark, all sharp angles and shadows. His grip on my breast loosened within minutes, and I heard his breathing begin to slow. I continued to rub his head, feeling his warm breath against my face, and I waited.

And waited.

And waited.

I wanted to be sure he was good and asleep before I dared move. There was no risk of me falling asleep as my mind raced. When an hour had passed without him moving, I slid his arm off my body and waited to see if he'd move. When he still didn't, I eased myself away from him, off the side of the bed, and then onto the floor. I crawled across my floor, the hardwood painful on my knees. When I made it to his pants, still on the floor where we'd left them, I pulled his phone free, turning down the brightness before I did anything else. I unlocked the phone and clicked on the app store button, searching for tracking apps. I couldn't remember the app my friend had used, but the first result seemed like it would work. I downloaded the app, watching as the purple icon appeared on his screen, and created an account for him. Then, I hid the app in a junk folder with a few of his other useless apps. I placed it somewhere in the middle of the apps, sure he'd never notice it there. Lastly, I sent myself a text message invite to join his circle, closed out of the app and locked his phone back, sliding it back into his pocket.

I stood, tiptoeing across the room and lifting my phone from the nightstand. I followed the same steps, downloading the app, and confirmed that I'd like to be in his circle. When I stared down at the final screen, we were two small circles, side by side at my address.

Next time I sent a picture, I'd know exactly where he was.

Next time he lied, I'd know the truth.

CHAPTER NINETEEN

NAOMI

Lucas arrived home an hour before our scheduled Sunday dinner with my parents. He hurried in the door, threw a hand over his head in a brief wave, and called out, "Sorry, I know I'm late. Surgery ran long. Be right back."

He rushed up the stairs, and I listened as his footsteps grew fainter. I turned to face Becca, waiting patiently at the table, and patted her seat. "Go ahead and get in your seat, sweet girl. I've got your plate ready. Grandma and Grandpa will be here soon."

She climbed up in the chair and I pushed it in and moved her plate toward her just as my phone chimed from across the room. I hurried over to where I'd laid it near the stove, lifting it and turning back to face Becca so I could keep an eye on her as she took a bite of her spanakopita.

The text was from my father.

Running late, sweetheart. We'll try to be there as soon as we can. You may have to start dinner

without us. I'll let you know if we won't make it. Xx.

I groaned, laying the phone down. It wasn't the first time they'd been late or failed to show up at all to a dinner we'd scheduled, and as they were preparing to travel to Bora Bora the next day, this was my last chance to see them for at least a month. Lucas entered the room, and I glanced up. He'd changed into more casual clothes, his polo tucked into khaki slacks, his hair brushed, and his tennis shoes traded for Doc Martens.

"How was work?" I asked, walking forward as he moved to approach me. He kissed my hairline, just above my ear, gripping my arm.

"Fine. I got put on a last-minute surgery that had some complications, which is why I'm late. I was worried I wouldn't beat your parents here."

I sighed, leading the way toward the table. "Well, they're running late apparently, so there was no rush."

His face fell. "Running late? Sweetheart, you worked so hard on all of this."

I nodded but didn't speak. He was right. I hadn't gone through this much trouble for a dinner in so long, but it had been years since we hosted my parents and I wanted them to be impressed. I hated that I felt that way. Like I needed to impress them or earn their approval. I'd worked so hard to build a life they were proud of, and still, they had so much power over me.

"It's almost too beautiful to eat," he said, eyeing the lamb on the platter in front of his seat.

"Well, thank you," I said, "but they said we should start without them, so I'm afraid it'll just be us who sees it."

"And me!" Becca cried gleefully.

"And you," I agreed, patting her arm.

He sank into his chair, staring at me. "We could wait..."

Becca took a bite of her food, chewing. She put another piece in her mouth, and I reached for her fork, much to her dismay. "Slow down, baby. One bite at a time or you'll choke."

"I won't choke," she argued.

Lucas laughed. "Well, someone's appreciating your food."

I offered a sad smile. "You're right." I lifted the knife, slicing us each a chunk of meat and placing them on our plates, then I added spanakopita next to the meat. Last, I put a scoop of salad on each of the plates and sighed. "Dig in, I suppose."

He reached across the table and took my hand, surprising me. "I'm sorry, babe. This is great. They're missing out." He seemed, like me, to already assume they weren't going to be showing up, further proof we'd done this song and dance before.

"Thanks," I said, taking a small bite of my lamb. I hated how pitiful I felt, how insignificant they could make me feel. It was only Lucas who saw it, but he understood better than anyone. Parents had never been our specialty. It was why we fit together so well. We understood each other in a way no person with a functional family could. Though our traumas were different, both our upbringings had damaged us beyond repair.

His finger rubbed across my knuckles. "It'll be okay. Once they're gone again, things'll be back to normal."

I looked at him, cocking my head to the side. "Is normal what we're striving for?"

He moved his hand back, taking a bite of salad. "Hm?"

"I mean, I know my parents being home adds a bit of stress to our lives, but even when they aren't here...do you think what we have is...I mean, are we good? Is *this* good?"

He scoffed, though his gaze was far-off, and he glanced around the room like someone was playing a prank on him. "Where is this coming from?"

"I just wondered, I guess. It feels like things have been so weird between us lately. I know you're working so much, and I don't blame you for that, I just..." I trailed off, unsure of where I was going or how to say what I truly wanted to say. It felt like we'd fallen apart. Like we were roommates, business associates who shared a bed but not much else. I had no idea what he did during the day anymore, though he used to share so much with me. "It feels like everything has changed."

"Nothing has changed," he said quickly, rubbing a hand across his jaw. "Why would you say that?"

I sucked in a breath. I desperately didn't want to fight, but I had to know the truth. No amount of searching Google for the phone number had pointed me in the right direction. "Who is A? In your phone?"

He placed his fork down, looking at his plate for a moment before looking back at me. "Who?"

"A. In your phone. The other night, when you'd gone downstairs there was a picture of a painting sent to your phone."

He pulled his phone from his pocket. "You're the one who deleted it?" he asked, his jaw tensing.

"Who was it? Who's A?" I asked again.

"*A* is Alexander Tremblay. He's an up-and-coming artist that does a lot of paintings downtown. I met him last week on my lunch break. He's a bright kid, but he's had a rough go of things. I thought we could help him out by buying a piece of his art. He was supposed to be painting something and sending it over, but I never got it. We saw each other again yesterday and he asked me if I didn't like it, but I had no idea what he was talking about. Why wouldn't you tell me?"

I sighed, feeling ridiculous. Of course there was an obvious explanation. "I thought...well, I don't know what I thought. It was a painting of a naked woman."

"And? Degas is your favorite artist. I hardly thought you'd be bothered by nudity."

"I'm not bothered by it," I argued swiftly. "I was just worried it meant more to you than a piece of art. It made me uncomfortable."

"More to me how, Naomi? It was a painting. I can't believe you went through my phone, let alone deleted a picture from it."

"I was worried you were cheating on me, okay? I wasn't trying to snoop, but you weren't in the bedroom and I wasn't sure if it was the hospital. When I saw the painting, and the fact that the sender didn't have a name in your contacts, I don't know, I just got jealous."

He scoffed, pushing away from the table. "*Cheating* on you, really? C'mon, you know me better than that. How could I? Between you two and work, I have no spare time."

"I know that," I said. "I just...it worried me."

He studied my face. "Have you been taking your medication?"

My jaw dropped, his question slamming into my chest. "Of course, I have. How can you even ask that?"

"You get paranoid when you're off your meds. It's a fair question. How can *you* ask *me* if I'm cheating?" He folded his arms across his chest, obviously angry.

"I'm sorry, Lucas, but I had to ask. I didn't say I don't believe you."

"Do you?"

I sucked in a breath. Truth was, I didn't know. I wanted to believe him, but his defensiveness made me feel wary. "I do, Lucas," I lied. "I do believe you. I was just feeling insecure." He stared at me, the tight line of his lips loosening.

"I'd never cheat on you. I'm not that guy."

I nodded. "I know you wouldn't. You wouldn't risk losing us." I threw the last sentence in carefully, just as it appeared his guard was down.

His eyes widened, his fingers flexing on the table. "I'd never want to lose you."

I gave a small smile and lifted my fork, though my appetite had all but disappeared. "Cheating is one thing I'd never tolerate, so I'm especially sensitive about it, you know? I'm sorry for jumping to conclusions."

"What do you mean you wouldn't tolerate it?" he asked, twisting his mouth. "It's not something anyone *tolerates*, is it? I mean, if it were to happen, we'd work through it and move past it. I'd be able to forgive you."

"What are you saying?" I placed my fork down again, a cool knot forming in my stomach.

"Nothing, I'm just talking, I guess." He broke his eye contact with me, taking another bite, though he was obviously shaken up.

I blinked, speaking calmly but with purpose. "If I ever found out you were cheating on me, I'd leave you in a heartbeat. There would be no fixing us and moving on. I don't operate that way, Lucas." I couldn't completely ignore the guilt in my heart, but rage and confusion outweighed it. *Is he cheating on me, after all?*

He looked up at me, his head cocked to the side. "You'd really break up our family?"

"You'd be the one breaking up our family, though, wouldn't you?" When he didn't answer, I pressed on. "Lucas, is there something you need to tell me?"

Lucas looked at Becca, and I followed his gaze, realizing she was staring at us intently. "What, Mama?"

I smiled, brushing a strand of hair from her eyes. "Nothing, sweetheart. Mommy and Daddy are just talking. Eat your food."

She pushed her meat around with her fork but didn't take a bite, and I returned my gaze to Lucas as he began to speak.

"I don't have anything to tell you because I've never cheated. But I don't think there's anything that would cause me to leave you and tear apart our family. I'm a firm believer that anything can be fixed."

I took another bite. "Well," I said, swallowing, "I guess

that's the difference between us, hm? I wouldn't fix something you chose to break."

"Well, you're right. I guess that *is* the difference, then." His tone had cooled considerably. "The problem being that *if* we were to separate, I'd be the one who'd end up with custody of Becca…"

Chills lined my skin. "How do you figure?"

"Well, with your history…of depression. I can't see how any judge would grant you custody over me."

"I can't believe you just said that to me," I said, feeling betraying tears fill my eyes. He blurred in my vision as he lifted his head to look at me. "My depression is completely under control. Has been for over a year. Mental illness is nothing to be ashamed of, Lucas. I've fought to get better, and I am."

"It's just facts, Nae. I'm not threatening you. I want us to be a family, but we both know if it weren't for me, we would've lost Becca after we had her when you had to be sent away."

"I was being treated for postpartum depression," I said through gritted teeth, anger boiling in my belly. "Don't make it seem like something it isn't. I did what was best for my health, and I'm all the better for it. I've been nothing but an excellent mom since then, and I'm furious that you're making me defend that right now." I paused, collecting myself. "Besides that, you're the one with such an insane schedule you only see your daughter for an hour or two a day, and that's on a good day. You're the one drowning in so much debt from before we met, my parents are paying most of our bills. How can you

possibly think you'd be the most stable parent?" I brushed
my tears away quickly, feeling ill.

"Well, I guess, if that situation were to ever present
itself, we'd just have to roll the dice then, wouldn't we?"
He took another slow bite, and I let out a haggard breath.
How had we gotten to this point? The dinner had started
off so well. I watched his expression as he stared at me,
chills running over my skin. For the first time in my
marriage, I didn't recognize the man sitting across from
me. I didn't recognize the fear that had settled into my
bones.

I took another bite, looking away and letting his
threats wash over me. Why was this happening? What was
he hiding? Why did the look in his eyes terrify me so
much?

I forced out a breath. "Yes, I guess we would. Luckily
for us, we'll never have to be in that position, will we?"

He smirked, his eyes pure stone. "Luckily for us, no we
won't."

CHAPTER TWENTY

CLARA

The knock on the door startled me, and I jumped, spilling hot tea into my lap. I cursed under my breath, standing up and placing the mug on the table as I reached for tissues to dab up the mess. I pulled my shirt away from my body, the hot liquid scalding my skin, and inhaled sharply through gritted teeth.

Ouch, ouch, ouch.

The front door burst open, reminding me of what had caused the burns in the first place, and I looked up, feeling pitiful at his confused face.

"What happened?"

"You scared me, that's what! I jerked with hot tea in my hand." The tea was rapidly cooling, though I was sure my legs and lower stomach would have first-degree burns.

"I'm sorry, Clara," Luke said, making his way toward me. He helped get the shirt over my head, pulling my pants down with a look of sheer concern. It was one I recognized, too, from the hospital. One that said he was all-consumed with his work. He looked over my legs, taking the tissues from my hand to dab up the rest of the mess. "It's okay. They're a bit red and painful, I'm sure, but it's not bad. We'll get you into a cool bath. Come on." He put a hand under my shoulder and ushered me into the guest bathroom down the hall.

"What were you knocking for, anyway?"

"I've told you, it's a habit." He shook his head as we reached the bathroom, and he helped me to rest against the sink.

"Honestly, I'm fine. I'll just get some aloe and ibuprofen. It's not so bad now. It was just a shock to the system."

He smirked but turned on the water in the bathtub anyway. "I'd still feel better if you had a cool soak first."

"Whatever you say, Doctor," I teased.

"Thank you, Doctor," he retorted, placing his hand under the faucet to check the temperature before lifting the lever to stop the water from draining. "In you go." He held out his hand and I placed mine in it as he led me across the small room and helped me sink into the rapidly filling water.

"Oh," I whispered, the cold water sending chills down my body. "Now see, this is just cruel."

He sank down beside the tub, keeping one arm inside the water and using his fingers to drip cool water on my sunburn-red upper thighs. "What's cruel is having to stare at you like this and knowing I can't touch you until the pain fades." He met my eyes, a hint of desire in their depths.

"I think I could suffer through the pain if you made it

worth my while," I teased, though I truly wasn't sure. *God, it hurts.*

His lips twisted in thought as he dropped more water onto my legs with his fingers before reaching up to turn off the faucet. I noticed his clothes for the first time. He was dressed in a polo, slacks, and dress shoes. "Special occasion?" I asked, raising a brow.

He glanced down at himself. "I just finished up dinner with Naomi and our parents, and as soon as it was done, I had to get out of there."

"Your parents?" I asked, shocked by his words. Far as I knew, he hadn't had contact with his mother in years, and I didn't think he even knew his father. "You didn't tell me you were back in touch."

His face fell, but quickly recovered. "Naomi set it all up. She's fine with them as long as they keep sending her money."

"*Money?*" Now I was sure I had it wrong. "I thought your mom was an addict who didn't have any money? Why did I think that? You said you were constantly having to send her money before... It was why you lost touch."

He shook his head, staring at me as if I'd lost my mind. Maybe I had. "You must be thinking of someone else. I've never had to send my mom money. *Trust me, my parents have plenty.* It just never gets spent on me, always Naomi. They don't have much to do with either of us, only when it's convenient for them, but Naomi's always been the favorite."

I shook my head, almost positive I'd had it right the first time. "So, if they send Naomi money, why do you have to take care of her? Why is she your responsibility?" I splashed a foot in the bathtub, drawing my attention away from him as I asked the question.

"I don't know. I guess I've always just felt like she's my responsibility. She's fragile, you know, and I'd never forgive myself if something happened to her."

"But she's not your responsibility, Lucas. She's taking advantage of your good nature. She knows you'll provide for her and Becca, and she doesn't have to work. Especially if your parents are sending her money, too. That responsibility isn't yours to shoulder. She's a grown woman." It was harsh, I knew. Aside from depression, and what I assumed but had never been told must be bipolar disorder, I didn't know the extent of Naomi's issues, but I knew that Lucas had been catering to them for far too long. From what he'd said, she was ungrateful for the sacrifices he made for her. She never said thank you or tried to help with bills while he was paying for everything, and she caused more problems than he could solve. I wanted so badly for Lucas to see that and finally realize it was time to ask her to leave. She was his sister and he loved her—I didn't have siblings so I'd never understand that bond completely, but I knew love and I knew how powerful it could be. Luke was the most loving man I knew, but I hated seeing him being taken advantage of.

"You're right, I know. I've actually been thinking a lot lately…"

"What do you mean?" I asked as his fingers slid slowly between my knees.

He rested his chin on the side of the tub, apparently

lost in deep thought. "What would you say if I asked you to run away with me?"

I snorted. The idea was preposterous, as if we were children ready to elope, but based on the serious expression on his face, I wasn't sure he was joking. "What are you talking about? Run away where?"

"Anywhere. Mexico. Canada. London. California. What if we just packed our bags and disappeared? Didn't show up for our next shift? Didn't tell anyone where we were going? What if we just drained our accounts and disappeared? Would you go with me?"

I chewed on my bottom lip, thinking over what he was saying. Just yesterday, he'd said he didn't like the idea of commitment beyond moving in together, and today he was all prepared to escape across the country with me. What had changed? "I don't know, Luke. I have a lease here, and...we love our jobs. Could you really give up being a surgeon?"

"We could be surgeons wherever we went. There are hospitals everywhere. And besides, I think I could give up everything for you... Can you say the same?"

I stared at him. It was all I'd wanted to hear for so long, but in that moment, it felt wrong. "You could give up on Naomi? Just like that? Becca? You'd leave them here?"

He nodded. "The only way I'll ever be rid of Naomi is if I can walk away from this town, from this life, and never look back. I want to build a life with you, Clara. You're the most real thing I've ever known, the best thing in my life, and after we talked last time, I guess it made me realize it. It made me realize I'm wasting time being without you."

"Where is this all coming from? It seems like a total one-eighty from where we were before."

He squeezed my thigh gently. "Naomi is just causing problems, as usual. I think it's time for us to part ways, but she'll never let me go if I stay here. We could move away, get a place set up, and then, if she still needs help with Becca, maybe she could come live with us."

I furrowed my brow, my body tensing at the thought. "Naomi?"

He scowled, moving his fingers through the water and holding them over my legs so the cool water dripped onto my burns. "God, no. I meant Becca."

"Naomi would give up her daughter?"

He shrugged, as if that was a normal thing to do. "I'm the one raising her. The one paying for everything she does. It'll only be a matter of time until I'm able to convince Naomi, or the courts if that's what it comes to, that I'm the best thing for her. Naomi's not well enough to care for Becca on her own."

I nodded, though if my thoughts had seemed harsh, his words seemed harsher. I knew Naomi had caused problems for him—too many to name—but I had no idea how to feel about his plan to take her child away from her. From all I'd seen and heard, he didn't seem particularly attached to the little girl and with our schedules, no matter the hospital, I didn't see how we could be fit parents either.

The possibilities raced through my mind. Would I be her mother? Not really, but an acting one anyway. Was I ready for that? I looked up at Luke, whose hopeful eyes hadn't left mine. With him, I felt everything was possible.

"You know I'd go anywhere with you, Luke. You're my home; you always have been." My heart thudded in my ears as I waited for him to respond. His grin grew wide and bright as his hand moved from my thigh to my hand where it rested on the side of the bathtub. He squeezed it gently, lifting it to his lips.

"I don't know why it took me so long to realize how much I love you."

I watched him carefully, wondering what exactly had happened at dinner to make things change so much between us. Whatever it was, I was grateful for the dramatic change in behavior. I was grateful to finally be on the same page. "Does this mean you're going to move in sooner?"

"It means I don't ever want to leave," he said. "As long as you'll have me."

"Forever," I whispered, sitting up and leaning toward his lips. I didn't care about the pain I felt, or the worry in my chest, I only cared about Luke. And, finally, he was all mine.

CHAPTER TWENTY-ONE

ALAINA

What are you doing, Lucas?

The dot on my phone screen led me to two different places that day. Once, to a large, brick home with oversized windows and an immaculate lawn. It was a far cry from the small, one bedroom he'd told me he lived in. He wasn't there long though, just an hour or two, but when he came out, he'd changed from his scrubs into a different outfit. Perhaps this was his parents' home? I had no way of knowing, but still, I followed. The more I watched, the more I would learn.

His next stop was at a small apartment complex across town. The street was crowded, but I eventually found a spot not too far away, where I could keep an eye on his car. He went down a quiet corridor, knocked once on the first door to the left, and then inserted his key and entered. It would make sense that this was his apartment, though I didn't know why he'd need to knock—maybe I'd seen wrong.

I waited, watching for movement. Why was this place

such a secret? Why wasn't I allowed to come here? To know where he lived? The apartment was quaint and cute in a busy, but safe, area. Sure, it wasn't exactly the kind of apartment I'd pictured him in. From what he'd said in the past, I thought he lived closer to the hospital, nearer where the first house was. I'd always imagined something more modern, with large windows like the first home, but sharper angles. Less homey and more bachelor pad. But this would work, too. It was much nicer than my apartment where we spent all of our time.

I watched his dot as it bounced back and forth around the apartment, occasionally showing up across the street and then coming back as it recalibrated. He was in there, for sure, and I was half tempted to show up, force myself in, and make him spill all of his secrets. Instead, I made myself practice patience. I needed to know what he was hiding.

IT WAS dark before there was movement outside of the apartment. I'd all but dozed off when I saw the outside light come on and watched him walk away. He was dressed back in his scrubs this time, ready for work, his face illuminated by the phone screen as he appeared to be typing a message.

He stopped outside of his car and glanced around. My heart sank as I tried to scoot further down in my seat. *Please no. Please no. Please no.* To my great relief, he pulled his keys from his pocket and climbed in the car, starting it up right away. If he'd seen me, he'd done an excellent job of hiding it. And why would he have to? Why was he hiding so much from me, and why hadn't I pushed to get these answers sooner? For so much of our relationship, I'd let Lucas lead blindly. He was older, wiser, and with more money and life experience. Who was I to try and push for things—answers—he was so unwilling to give me. He was nearly twice my age, rich, and he loved me, so I didn't care about the rest. He was good to me. But now, with the baby coming, I had to know the truth about the man I was going to be marrying.

After his car had pulled out of the parking lot, I backed out of my own parking spot and followed in the direction he'd turned, doing my best to keep my distance. It was dark, so I was sure he couldn't make out my car even if he noticed me, but I didn't want to chance him worrying about being followed.

He turned onto the interstate a few miles up, and I sped up, worried about losing him from where I was. I entered the interstate just as he merged across two lanes, directly behind a semi, with another behind him. I had no way to cut in safely. I crossed the lanes after the semi, with eyes no longer on him. I sped up, trying to make sure I stayed close to him, but to my surprise, the car was no longer between the semis. He'd gotten over, but into which lane? I searched the dark interstate, nothing but headlights and taillights, looking for his car. *Where did you go?*

I sped up again, then slammed on my brakes as a minivan with a busted taillight cut me off. I cursed, slamming a hand on the steering wheel. He was gone. I'd lost him.

I pulled off at the next exit, unsure where I was. Had he seen me, after all? Was that why he'd been driving so erratically? Or maybe it was my imagination.

I lifted my phone from the center console, ready to type my address into the GPS to get home, then I froze. How had I forgotten? I could still track him.

I'd lost focus and forgotten about my new trick.

I stared at the dot, zooming in to get a good idea of where he was. He'd gotten off the interstate two exits ahead of me. I clicked the button on the app that gave me directions to his location, ever changing as he moved, and placed it on the console again, my eyes trained on the screen.

I pulled out and turned right. *If you thought you could lose me that easily, you've underestimated me.*

I grinned to myself, proud of my quick thinking. He couldn't escape me this time. I was going to get my answers.

Fifteen minutes later, I checked the locks on my doors as I pulled into an unfamiliar area of town. There were bars on windows and street lights that had burned out. What would Lucas be doing here?

I drove slowly, my heart thudding in my chest as my nerves amplified. On the corner, I spied a group of young men, younger even than I was. They stood still, hands in their pockets as they watched my car closely. I swallowed, keeping steady on the road until they were out of sight. Lucas' dot had turned on a street just up ahead, and he appeared to be stopped.

With growing apprehension, I turned right, slowing as I neared his dot. Sure enough, his car was parked on the street, though it was dark, and I couldn't see him inside of it.

What are you doing here, Lucas?

What is this place?

I looked up at the buildings around us. A small market was to my left, with trash gathered outside of it. There was an overweight man inside, standing behind the counter. He glanced out the window as I drove past. Up above the market were two small apartments, with balconies and fire escapes, though they both looked to be empty or turned in for the night, with newspapers taped on their windows.

To the right, there was a rundown apartment building with window units in each window and two lion sculptures with graffiti covering their exterior at the entrance.

I glanced at his car as I drove past it. It was definitely empty. Wherever Lucas was, I couldn't be sure. I stepped on the gas as two shadowy figures came out of an alley, a bulky man and a woman severely underdressed for the crisp fall weather. I needed to get out of there. I forced out a breath, trying to slow my shaking hands as I turned onto the next street, stopped at a stop sign, and then sped out of town.

Lucas' little purple dot was haunting me as I moved further away, but I couldn't stay. I could hardly breathe as I pushed the pedal further, seeing the sign for the interstate up ahead. I had to get back to safety. For now, whatever his secrets were, they were his to keep.

CHAPTER TWENTY-TWO

NAOMI

The fight with Lucas had taken place hours before, but still, I couldn't shake the feeling of unease. There had been a coldness in his eyes that I didn't recognize. Sure, we'd had our troubles. Things hadn't been perfect between us in a long time, but this was different. *He* was different. A chill ran over me, causing the hair on my arms to stand on end as I thought about it.

From my laptop, I closed out of Facebook and opened my online banking site. It had been too long since I'd checked the account, and after what he'd said about taking Becca and about me being unfit, I wanted to make sure there was no validity to those statements. I was going to make sure I was on top of everything. The account was set up so that my parents' money came into it on the fifteenth of every month and then on the first, all of our bills were auto-drafted. Set it and forget it had always been the easiest way for me, and Lucas' income was just an extra cushion.

I typed in the login and scrolled. Electric, gas, water,

AmEx, Netflix…I stopped. *Waters and Flagstaff Prop $688.* What was that? I scrolled down a bit more. Our land-scapers payments came out under something similar, but it was nowhere near that high to my recollection.

There it was.

Not all that similar in fact. *Waterstone's Lawn Care, LLC Pay.*

I went to Google and searched Waters and Flagstaff Properties. They were out of Ohio, but it looked as though they had a few properties all over the Southeast and Midwest. I scrolled down a bit more. Every month on the third, going back six months—and that was just as far as my history would take me. I pulled up a statement from nine months ago. Ten. A year ago. Eighteen months. They were always on there. Nearly seven hundred dollars a month.

I went back to the transaction, noting the last four digits of the card that had authorized it. I stood and hurried across my bedroom, digging in my purse and retrieving my wallet. I pulled out the gold card with blue lettering, and studied the last four numbers. They weren't mine.

I went back to the account and pulled up the cards associated with our banking, focusing on the card with the four digits that matched the rent payment. I selected the button that would reveal the entire card number and wrote it down, just in case the bank's site logged me out due to inactivity. Then, I turned back to Google and called the headquarters for the company, pressing my way through the prompts to get to an actual human.

"Thanks for contacting Waters and Flagstaff, where

luxury is home. Just as a reminder, this call may be monitored or recorded for quality assurance. May I have your first and last name please?" she asked, not introducing herself.

"Yes, my name is Naomi Martin," I told her, my hands shaking as I gripped the phone in my hand.

"Nice to speak to you today, Ms. Martin. What can I do for you?"

"I'm calling about an account that my card has been paying for several months now, but I'm not sure what it's to. If I give you the card number, are you able to give me any information?"

She paused. "Um, I'm not sure. Do you have any idea what property the account is with? We have sixty-seven in total."

"I don't...I'm sorry."

"What about the city or state? That might help me narrow it down a bit? I'd have to search the card number by individual property and that may take some time."

"Well, I'm in Nolensville, Tennessee, but I'm not positive that's where the payments are being made. We may have been hacked."

"Okay, the closest property we have to Nolensville... looks like, would be Nashville. We have three properties in Nashville I can check for you," she said, and I could hear her typing. "What's the rent amount?"

"It's for six hundred eighty-eight."

She was typing again. "Okay, that narrows it down again. Looks like two of the three properties are all well over a thousand at a minimum. So, we're looking at our Gardner Apartments on North Creek. Okay," she paused, "now, let's get that card number and I'll see what I can find."

I recited the card number to her and waited as she repeated it back to me. "What did you say your last name was?"

"Martin," I told her.

"There it is. Looks like the account is under Lucas Martin. Anyone you know?"

My body went cold. "Yes, that's my husband."

I heard her take a breath, but she didn't immediately speak. "I can give you the address." There was a sense of urgency there, woman to woman. "If—if that would help."

"That would help tremendously," I said, no power left in my voice.

"It's not really in our policy, but the card is in your name..." She trailed off, obviously nervous.

I didn't want to lie, but it was hardly stretching the truth. "Yes, it is. I wouldn't want to get you in trouble. I'm sure my husband's renting the place for a friend of his. He's always trying to help out."

"Okay, here's what I have on file for *your* address, Ms. Martin." She recited the address to me, and I jotted it down, clicking the pen when I was finished.

"Thank you so much," I told her. "Truly."

"You're very welcome. It's what I would want someone to do for me. I wish you luck with...everything. Is there anything else I can do for you tonight?"

"That'll be it. Thank you again." I ended the call and took a deep breath, staring at the address scrawled across the notebook page. Whose rent were we paying? Why hadn't Lucas told me?

I stared at my phone. There was one person who might be able to answer my questions, but I desperately didn't want to call him. I weighed my options, which were extremely limited, and eventually sighed. What choice did I have? Confront Lucas? If he were hiding it, he'd find a way to lie his way through it anyway.

I scrolled through my contacts and clicked on his name, squeezing my eyes shut as I lifted the phone to my ear. He answered almost immediately, as if he were waiting for my call.

"Hello?"

"Hey…" There was so much weight in that pause, so much of the unknown. We hadn't spoken since…

"I'm surprised you're calling. Everything okay?"

I nodded, my chest tight. "Yeah, um, sorry. I know I've been quiet lately, I just—"

"Didn't know what to say? Yeah, I got that," he said, and to my great relief, there seemed to be a playful hint to his tone. "I just assumed you needed space. Or that you hated me."

"I could never hate you, Brent. You know that."

"Do I?"

"Well, you should," I lied. What reason had I ever given him to know that? *I can think of at least two…*

He cleared his throat. "I'm assuming there's a reason for your call."

Getting back to business, I clicked the pen in my hand, tracing over the address absentmindedly. "Actually, there is. I… This is going to sound terrible. Lucas and I had a, er, well, we had an argument this afternoon, where divorce got brought up, and he was…well, anyway, long story short, I found a few transactions on our statements that I'm not recognizing. They're for an apartment complex north of downtown, nearly seven hundred dollars a month. Do you have any idea what that might be?"

He inhaled sharply through his teeth, and I could suddenly hear the wind in his speaker. He'd stepped outside. Had I interrupted something? "I wish I did, but with my brother, there's honestly no telling. Did you get the address?"

"Yeah," I said, unable to hide the disappointment from my voice. "I mean, we could've been hacked, I guess. Is it bad that that's what I'm hoping for? But the account is listed under his name. Do you think he has an apartment I don't know about? Would he? I mean, what could he need one for? To get away from me?" The answer was there, though it made no sense. Obviously, without me realizing it, our marriage had gotten bad enough that he needed a reason to hide out from me. Was I truly so miserable to live with?

"You know I wouldn't put anything past Lucas," he said, venom in his tone. "He's always been a liar, Naomi. I know you love him, and I truly do think he loves you, but…in the end he only cares about—"

"Himself. Yeah, I know." I'd heard this speech from Brent more times than I could count. The brothers were a true Cain and Abel story—nothing but pure hatred between them. Their only connection was me, something I'd once been proud of, but now I wasn't sure what to feel. Far as I knew, Cain and Abel hadn't been in love with the same woman. "Well, I suppose I could just head down there and see. Maybe this is all just a misunderstanding."

"Go to the apartment, you mean?"

"Sure, why not?"

"No way in hell are you going to any apartment alone," he said with a scoff. "If you're insistent on going, you're taking me with you."

"You don't have to do that, Brent. You have work. I'm a big girl, you know? And besides, if it is just Lucas, what have I got to worry about?"

He didn't say anything at first, and I heard the wind pick up again through the line. "It's going to storm tonight. I'll come by the house in the morning. You can text me when he's gone, if you want." He paused. "Naomi, I need you to swear you won't go alone."

"I swear, I won't. I really appreciate the help, Brent. I wouldn't ask if it wasn't important."

"You aren't asking me. I'm telling you. Whether it's Lucas or not, we both know you discovering this apartment could put you in danger. Can you get a sitter for Becca in the morning?"

"I think danger is a bit extreme, but sure. I can get a sitter for her. You can come by whenever in the morning, you don't have to wait for my text. Lucas is gone for the night, and he took a bag. He'll be staying at the hospital." A strange thought washed over me, but I didn't dare speak it aloud. Perhaps he was staying at his secret apartment instead.

"Must've been some fight..." He let out a laugh under his breath.

135

"You know Lucas. Always one to make things interesting." I smiled sadly, though he couldn't see it.

"That's my brother," he said wryly. "Are you going to be okay for the night?"

"I'll be fine," I told him, just as I heard Becca crying from down the hall. "I should go, anyway. I'll see you tomorrow?"

"See you tomorrow," he confirmed. "Call me if you need anything."

"Always," I promised, then I let the phone slip from my ear. Why was it so easy to call on the man whose ring I didn't wear?

CHAPTER TWENTY-THREE

CLARA

When Luke left for work in the middle of the night, I couldn't shake the feeling that something worse than what he'd told me happened had happened. It wasn't my business, I knew. I kept warning myself I should stay out of it. As much as I wanted Luke all to myself, I didn't want him if it meant hurting him in the long run. I had to know what happened with Naomi, why he was suddenly so willing to leave her.

To get the answers I needed, I had to go directly to the source.

Luke would kill me if he knew what I was planning. Luckily for me, he'd never have to know. If Rena in payroll thought it was strange that I'd called looking for Luke's address the next morning, she didn't let on, especially not after I told her it was because we were chipping in for his birthday next week and I was having his gift delivered. When I'd asked if she'd pitched in her portion yet, she'd all but thrown his address at me, in a hurry to get off the phone. If there was one thing you could count on Rena for, it was skipping out on hospital potlucks, birthday pools, or gifts for the chief.

I pulled into the driveway of a large brick house, glancing around for any sign of a child's toys, but I didn't see any. Didn't Becca play outside? I exited my car, noticing the cherry red Grand Prix in the driveway parked in front of the garage. What was I going to say to Naomi when I met her? I wrung my hands together in front of me, sweat beading at my hairline as I tried to think of what to say, what to do, how to introduce myself. It wasn't as if we were meeting under the best of circumstances.

Hey, Naomi. It's me, your brother's girlfriend. I'm here to ask if you've recently harmed your daughter or given Luke any reason to want to run away and take her with us?

Somehow, it was lacking.

I forced my hands to my sides, adjusting my blouse as I sucked in a haggard breath. I could do this. I was good with people. Good with awkward situations. I'd make the best of this and then, somehow, some way, I'd make Luke understand why it had to be done.

It was well past time.

I made my way up the walk and toward the front step, raising my fist to knock on the thick, mahogany door. Within seconds, I could hear footsteps headed my way.

This was it.

I was going to meet her.

The woman I'd heard stories about for twelve years.

The woman I knew so much about, yet I still didn't know what she looked like.

The woman I was competing with for my boyfriend, despite her inability to actually date him.

The woman who terrified me more than I liked to admit.

The woman I desperately wanted to like me.

The door swung open, and I took in the sight of the woman—stretch of a word there, it seemed. She looked thirty years younger than me at least. She stood in front of me, chestnut brown hair cut just above her shoulders, wearing a lime green T-shirt and blue jeans with scuffed up sneakers. There was scrutiny in her gaze as she studied me from inside the house, brushing a piece of hair behind her ears.

"Can I help you?"

"Yes, hello. I'm...I'm Clara DeVoss. You've probably heard a bit about me." I tried to laugh. With Luke, it was a toss-up. She either knew my entire life story, or she'd been unable to get a word about me out of him.

She stared at me blankly before shaking her head, and I realized it must have been the latter. Surely she at least realized who I was. In the background, I heard a little girl giggle loudly. "You're missing it!" she cried.

The woman turned, calling over her shoulder, "Be right there, sweetie." When her gaze returned to meet mine, she took half a step back. "Sorry. What were you saying?"

"Sorry, I should've mentioned I'm the girlfriend. From the hospital. Anyway, I'm sorry to bother you without giving you a heads up that I'd be coming, but I didn't have a way to contact you. I actually just wondered if we could talk. I know Luke is at work. Truth be told, he'd probably be upset with me for coming, but I've been dying to meet you. I suppose you have some questions for me, too."

"I'm sorry," the woman shook her head again, "I think you must be confused. Are you looking for Mrs. Martin?"

My heart sank. "Are you not Naomi?"

The woman chuckled, much to my mortification. "I'm Rianne, Becca's sitter. Mrs. Martin stepped out for the morning to run a few errands, but she should be back this afternoon. Would you like me to leave a message for her when she returns?"

I took a step back, nearly tripping on the small half-step in front of their door. *All of this for nothing.* "No, sorry. I must have sounded like a lunatic. I should've checked who you were before I started babbling. It's just...I've never met Naomi. Luke's told me all about her, but...well, like I said, he wouldn't be happy I'm here. He's incredibly protective of his sister. I'm sure you under-stand why."

The girl's face changed from cheerful to confused. "Sorry, his...his sister?"

"Yes, right. Talking about Naomi, of course. You'd think he'd want to introduce us, but men, you know—" I was babbling, my face growing red-hot with embarrass-ment as I couldn't seem to stop the flow of word vomit.

"You think Naomi is Mr. Martin's *sister*?" She wrinkled her nose with apparent disgust, and the blood drained from my face, no longer red-hot.

"Well...isn't she?" She seemed not to want to answer, so I encouraged her. "I could have it wrong."

"I'm sorry, I really shouldn't get involved," she said, taking a step back.

"Rianne, please..." I put my hand on the door as she moved to shut it. "Please just tell me." Her eyes were wide with fear as I pulled my hand from the door. "Sorry."

"Naomi and Lucas are married," she said, gripping the door with both hands. "I'm not sure where you heard differently, but they've been married for as long as I've known her, which is just over four years. Lucas doesn't have any sisters, to my knowledge. I think he has a brother or two, but I'm not positive." She drew in one side of her mouth in a pitiful expression.

"Right," I said, feeling like a hole had been torn through my insides. Her words were only being halfway processed. How was it possible? It wasn't, and yet here we were. The answer to all my questions. Why he was so apprehensive to move forward. Why he was so secretive about his life. Why he couldn't walk away from Naomi.

I am the other woman.

The man I loved with all my heart was splitting his heart between two women. Did he love her more? She'd gotten the ring, after all. And the house. And the child.

"I should really go back inside now. Becca doesn't like to be alone for too long. Should I...er, I mean, I could leave a message that you dropped by."

"No," I said, too quickly, then smiled. "No. That won't be necessary. I'm sorry to have bothered you, Rianne." I stumbled backward, unable to meet her eyes as my vision blurred with fat tears. What had I done?

"No bother," the woman whispered, seeming relieved to be done with the conversation. She closed the door, leaving me to my racing thoughts. I turned around, adrenaline coursing through me as I hurried back to my car, half aware that I seemed to have no control over my body or my movements. I was filled with an odd combination of rage and devastation, no idea which emotion to act on first.

I didn't want to believe it.

I wanted it to all have been a bad dream.

It had been, right?

What was the alternative?

If what she'd said was true, our entire relationship had been a lie. I refused to believe that. Luke wouldn't do that to me.

He loved me, didn't he?

CHAPTER TWENTY-FOUR

ALAINA

I met Lucas at the door.

Surprise, surprise, he'd given me no warning he was coming. Again.

"Going somewhere?" he asked, eyeing the purse in my hand and my made-up face.

"What tipped you off?" I turned around, locking the door behind me and moving past him down the hall.

"Hang on a moment," he said, reaching for my arm and spinning me back around. "Am I missing something? Are you mad at me?"

"Why would you think that?" I asked, twisting my lip ring with my tongue. I'd had it out for the past few days, so it was a weird sensation, wearing it again.

"Because of the way you're acting. Did I do something wrong?"

I shook my head. "I don't know. Did you?"

"Of course I didn't. Not to my knowledge, anyway. When I left, things were pretty great between us."

"You left before I'd even woken up Sunday morning. I

didn't hear from you all day yesterday, and you just show up randomly today and assume I don't have plans? Where were you, Lucas?"

His jaw dropped and relief filled his face. "Is that what this is about? I'm sorry." His fingers wrapped around my forearm. "I should've called. I got called in for a surgery and stuck on two twelve-hour shifts. I didn't even leave the hospital until just now."

"Just now?" I ran my gaze over his fresh scrubs.

"Yes, honestly." He held up two fingers. "First chance I had, I hurried over to see you. I hated leaving while you were asleep, but I didn't want to wake you." I felt him pulling me toward him, but I wasn't giving in. He didn't know he'd been caught in a lie, and I wasn't ready to show my cards yet. "I've missed you."

I leaned forward, but only barely. Enough for him to brush his lips on my cheek. "I'm running late for a doctor's appointment. Do you want to come?"

He glanced at my stomach. "For the baby?"

"Mhm," I said, putting a protective hand over my stomach. "There'll be an ultrasound. It's the first time you'll get to see her."

His eyes bugged out. "Her?"

"Wishful thinking," I teased. "You don't have to come if you don't want to." I turned away, ready to leave, but he jogged to catch up with me.

"No, I want to. I'm coming." His gesture surprised me, but I couldn't allow myself to get too caught up in his nicety. He was lying. For whatever reason, he didn't want me to know what he'd been doing last night. *Who* he'd been doing for all I knew.

"Okay, fine," I said. "Let's go, then. I don't want to be late."

We rushed out to the car, him trying to slow me down as we descended the stairs, citing a fear that I'd trip and fall, though I wasn't sure that wasn't actually wishful thinking on his part. I felt tears in my eyes at the thought, but I brushed them away before climbing in the driver's seat. He reached for my hand in the car, but I kept them firmly at ten and two. I had no interest in playing whatever game he was trying to play with me. We were playing my own game now, he just didn't realize it.

We rode in nearly complete silence the whole forty-five-minute drive. Once, when he'd tried to speak, I turned up the radio, claiming whatever song was playing just happened to be my favorite.

When we arrived at the hospital, he shook his head. "I still don't know why you insist on going to the doctor here rather than closer to your place. When you're in labor, you're not going to want to make this drive."

"Well, when I picked it, I thought I was doing you a favor by finding a doctor close to your work, since that's where you always seem to be. Is Dr. Montgomery not any good? I've really liked her so far."

"No, Alexa's great," he said, though his face was pale and ashen. Ordinarily, I'd have thought it was because he was nervous for the appointment. This time, though, I knew the truth, and I was mentally high-fiving my former self for picking this office for my prenatal care. If he was going to lie about being at work, I was going to make that as difficult as possible for him.

Lucas and I had very different goals as we walked

across the crowded parking lot and through the double, automatic doors. I hoped more than anything to run into a coworker of his that I recognized. If I knew Lucas, he was going to attempt to make sure I didn't.

The sterile smell hit me right away, and I slowed down as a nurse wheeled an elderly lady in a wheelchair past me, talking slowly to her as they made their way into the elevator. I turned left, toward the stairwell, and headed for the third floor.

"You're taking the stairs?" he asked, trying to keep up with me.

"I always do. I need my steps."

"You're pregnant. I think you can afford to miss a few steps."

"I'll take my doctor's advice, thanks," I snapped back.

"Are we okay?" he asked, stopping for a moment, but when I didn't, he continued on.

"We're fine, Lucas. I just want to get to the appointment."

He sighed, not believing me, but forced to carry on anyway.

For once, we were on the same page.

Fifteen minutes later, I'd checked in and the nurse called us back. Lucas waited outside while I gave my urine sample, and then we stepped into the room where the ultrasound tech was waiting.

"Hi, Alaina," she said, giving a half-wave in the semi-lit room. "Go ahead and hop up here on the bed for me." Her eyes followed Lucas as he took a seat on the far wall. "You must be Dad?"

He nodded, but looked down without a word. She

seemed a bit taken aback but didn't let it throw her off. Instead, she turned her attention to me once again. "Is this your first time seeing your little one?"

I swallowed, my attention momentarily diverted as I realized this was really happening. I was finally going to see the little life I'd been growing. "Yes."

"How exciting," she said, lifting my shirt to just below my breasts. "This gel will be a little warm. They like that." She grinned, squirting the gel onto my lower belly and lifting the transponder. "You're a little over nine weeks, it looks like, so we're probably just going to see a small little bean today. We'll make out some body parts if we're lucky, but mostly, it won't look like anything at all. And if we don't hear the heartbeat, don't panic. It may be too early still, but we should be able to see it beating."

I nodded, trying to swallow down the ginormous lump in my throat as she placed the probe onto my stomach. She pressed down harder than I'd expected, and I watched the screen fill with white fuzz. She moved the transponder around on my belly, pushing and poking, though I couldn't make out anything—

There she was. He. She. Whoever.

My baby.

Our baby.

It was there. Very much like a bean, though I could make out the smallest little head and an arm. There might have even been a foot in there.

"There's baby," she said, pointing at the screen. "You can see the cord here. And the head." She moved her finger across the screen as she spoke. "There's the little hand and you can see—oh, he's wiggling. See?"

I nodded, embarrassed by the tears suddenly in my eyes as the bean moved back and forth, its little hips swaying side to side.

"Perfectly healthy size," she said as her mouse moved across the screen taking measurements. "And there's the placenta here. He's snuggled up against it. You can see the heartbeat, too." She zoomed in a bit. "Let's see if we can hear." She adjusted the transponder as I waited with bated breath. The room filled with the whooshing sound I'd heard on the many YouTube videos I'd researched. It sounded right. Perfect. Healthy. "Strong heartbeat. One fifty-four. Right where we want it to be."

I smiled, proud of the heartbeat I'd created, and looked over at Lucas. My heart sank as I saw him staring down at his phone, not spending even a moment taking in our child. When I looked back, the interaction hadn't gone unnoticed by the tech, who offered me a reassuring smile.

She froze the screen centered on the baby, typing, "Hi Mom!" next to its tiny arm and pressing a button. I heard the picture print from the machine next to me as she pushed down a bit harder. "We just need to get a few measurements for your doctor and I'll be done prodding on you. Everything looks great, though. Are you hoping for a boy or a girl?"

I looked to Lucas again, feeling devastated when he still couldn't be bothered to look back at me.

"Healthy, right? That's all that really matters," the tech answered for me, when I couldn't respond through my tears. "It's all going to be okay, Mama." Her smile was small and sad, as if she knew Lucas' and my story, as if she'd seen it before. But there was no way she could've. *I* didn't even know our story.

I tried to smile back, refusing to give Lucas a second look as she finished the ultrasound, giving me one last peek at my baby before she shut it off. She handed me the images she'd printed off and dried my belly, handing me a paper towel to clean what she'd missed.

"These images are being scanned to your doctor right now, so she can go over everything with you. Once you're cleaned up, just step right out into the hall and they'll get you into a room, okay?"

I nodded, wiping away the excess jelly.

"Good luck, Alaina. And congratulations."

"Thank you," I said, and I couldn't remember if she'd told me her name or not, so instead of saying it when I felt I should've, I just repeated, "Thank you."

As she closed the door, Lucas looked up at me finally. There was no apology in his eyes, and I knew there was nothing but devastation in my own.

"Do you want to see?" I heard myself asking, though I didn't want to do it.

He stood, not taking a step toward me. "I saw already, babe. She said it's healthy. That's good."

"You weren't watching, Lucas. I saw you."

He shook his head. "Yes, I was. I saw it."

"Do you even care?" I asked, my voice breaking. I shoved the photos toward him, forcing him to look at them. He swallowed, refusing.

"Of course I care, Alaina."

"But you'd rather we didn't have the baby, wouldn't you?"

He scoffed, his brow furrowing. "What are you talking about?"

"You don't want to do this…do you? You don't want to have this baby."

"Well, it's a little late for that."

He wasn't denying it. "It's not. I could have an abortion. I'm still under the limit."

I wanted him to say I was crazy. To beg me not to joke like that. To tell me he'd seen the same miracle I had. Instead, his face grew very serious. "I can't make that decision for you."

"But you would, if it were up to you? You'd tell me to have the abortion?"

"I haven't thought about it," he said softly, finally looking at the screen, though it was blank this time.

"Well, think about it, Lucas. Tell me what it is you want."

"I want you," he said quickly. "I want what we have."

"*What we have* is a child growing in my stomach. A child that will be here in a matter of months. Now, if you don't want to help me raise it, I need to know right away. So I can make that decision alone."

"You know I'll be there for you if you decide to keep the baby."

I brushed a tear away from the corner of my eye. "But you'd rather I didn't?"

He sighed, dropping his head. "Are you going to make me say it, Alaina? Really?"

"I'm not making you say anything," I told him, my stomach twisting as I prepared myself for what I knew was coming.

"Would it be easier? Yes. Is it going to be really hard raising a kid when we are still getting to know each other? Yes. Would I rather have waited until we were married and settled? Yes."

"Would you like me to get an abortion?" I forced the question out through gritted teeth.

His gaze remained locked with the floor. "Yes."

I choked out a sob, and he looked up, reaching for me. "I still want to marry you," he told me, pressing his forehead against my temple as his arms held me tight. I felt like I couldn't breathe. I didn't want him near me. Didn't want to breathe in his smell. Didn't want to be held by him, yet I couldn't move. I was frozen by fear and grief, locked in place as I tried to decide whether to scream or sob or vomit. "I still want to marry you and start our lives together, I just want to get the timing right. This pregnancy will complicate it all."

I nodded, barely, and stood up from the bed, my body stiff. "You should go."

"No, don't do—"

"I think you should go, Lucas, now." I pushed his arm off my shoulder, slinking away from him.

"Alaina, please—"

"I'll schedule the appointment for the abortion, but I don't want you there." The words made me sick to my stomach, but I resisted the urge to touch my bump. "It was a mistake bringing you with me."

"Don't say that…"

"I want you to go, Lucas. Now," I repeated, moving toward the door. I was going to be sick or pass out, but I wasn't sure which, or in which order.

"You shouldn't be alone for this."

"I'm used to being alone," I spat. "Just please...I can't be with you right now."

"Should I call a cab and wait for you at your place?"

My place. After all that talk of moving in together, it was still mine. Just another of his lies. "I think it'd be best if you went to your own place for a while."

"For the night?"

"Forever, Lucas. I don't want to see you anymore."

"You don't mean that—" His expression fell, and he reached for me again.

"I do. I really, really do."

A knock sounded at the door, and I heard the tech's voice come through. "Everything okay in there?"

Lucas looked at me with panic in his eyes. "Please..." he begged.

I let out a slow, steady breath through my lips, trying to remain calm. "Please just go."

As the door opened, Lucas gave in, hanging his head and scurrying past the worried-looking tech. She took one look at my face and moved toward me, her arms around me without a word.

I let her hold me as I cried, as I finally allowed myself to put my arms around my growing belly, and as I contemplated my next move. Whatever it would be, I'd be making it alone.

CHAPTER TWENTY-FIVE

NAOMI

We sat in my parked car, waiting. For what, I wasn't sure. I needed to know the truth, my heart was begging for it, and yet, I couldn't move. Beside me, Brent sat quietly. His steel gray eyes were locked ahead, not meeting mine, and occasionally, he ran a hand over his dark beard. He smelled of grease and aftershave, an odd combination for anyone but a mechanic. On him, it was just his scent. One I knew well, one that I loved.

He crossed his arms over his chest, sucking in a sigh. He was waiting for me to say something, and I knew I should, but I couldn't bring myself to speak. What were we going to discover here? What secret of Lucas' had I managed to uncover?

I cleared my throat but couldn't come up with anything new to say, so instead, I pushed open my door and stepped out of the car. Brent was out in an instant, and I locked the door twice, very aware of the fact that this side of town may not be the safest.

The building was rundown, a few windows on the lower floor broken, most left that way while a few had been *repaired* with cardboard and duct tape. Brent moved closer to me, slowing his gait to make sure he was right next to me.

"You okay?" he grunted.

I nodded, though I was anything but, and we both knew it. His arm brushed mine, but he did nothing else, keeping our bodies close as we moved up the stone staircase. He reached for the door as I did, and I mumbled a quick *thank you* and stepped into the musty building. It smelled of smoke and ammonia, the floor a dingy yellow. I shuddered as the glass door closed behind us, sealing our fate. We were really doing this.

"Try as I might, I just can't picture Lucas in a place like this," I whispered, surprised when his hand wrapped around my wrist. There was nothing romantic about the gesture, it was pure protection, but my stomach filled with fire regardless. The last time he'd touched me, we'd made a terrible mistake.

He curled his lip. "Me either. Are you sure about this? It's not too late to turn around." He kicked a piece of what looked like tire rubber away from his shoe, looking around the building with disgust.

"I have to know," I told him, waiting for his approval.

He nodded, lowering his hand slightly, so our fingers were interwoven. Our gazes latched onto one another, and I wanted to say so much. My chest swelled with all that was unspoken between us in that moment, but instead of saying any of it I pulled him toward the stairs, and together, we walked up the faded, dingy, carpeted stairs toward the third floor. On the second, I could hear a couple arguing through the paper-thin walls. A skinny, blue-eyed, young boy sat in the hall, pushing a toy car that was missing a wheel.

I started to say something to him, offer him more than a smile, but Brent squeezed my hand, shaking his head and pushing me to keep moving. His eyes were stone, his expression blank as we arrived on the third floor. The sun shone in through the window, warming my skin in the already-warm hallway.

"Three-oh-four," I said, pointing to the second apartment on our right. *This is it.* We approached the nicotine-stained door, and I took a deep breath, exhaling sharply through O-shaped lips. I looked at Brent, who stared back at me with a stern expression. He gave a slight jerk of his head and stepped halfway in front of me.

His fist lifted to the wood of the door and he rapped against it three times, then stepped back, a hand out to push me even further behind him. I wondered if he could hear the way my heart was racing.

After several long minutes, he lifted his hand to the wood again, this time knocking with more force. He glanced over his shoulder at me, looking disappointed. What would we do if no one answered? What was next? I looked up at the peephole. If Lucas was just on the other side of that door, would he answer? Was he watching us right then?

I drew in my lips, biting down as I contemplated the possibilities. I couldn't let myself get overwhelmed just yet.

Finally, I heard a noise from somewhere inside the apartment. A loud *thump.*

We stepped back even further in unison, until I could feel myself getting too close to the wall behind me. Brent's hand was still in front of me, as if his palm and five outstretched fingers could shield me from whatever was on the other side of that door.

I listened as a chain lock was loudly removed, then another. The deadbolt clicked. The door knob clicked. He looked at me, both our expressions sheer fear and apprehension. We turned our heads toward the door as it swung open.

A wrinkled hand emerged first, pressed onto the front of the door, the other on the door frame. When she stepped into view, I saw the white hair and wrinkled, sallow face. Her eyes were empty shells, dark sores on her face, and half of her top teeth were missing.

I had no idea who I was staring at, but to my surprise, she seemed to know me. Her smile was small and smug as she darted her gaze from me to Brent. She took another small step forward, still holding onto the wall as if it was the only thing holding her up.

Beside me, Brent was still as stone. He sucked in a shallow breath, his hand moving to touch me as a strong, pungent smell of body odor and animal feces filled the hall.

She clicked her tongue. "Hello, Brent."

I looked at him, waiting for an answer, but his expression hadn't changed in the slightest. He was utterly emotionless as he muttered the words that shook me to my core. He pushed me forward and further away as he said them, seeming to be unable to get us away quickly enough.

"Goodbye, Mom."

CHAPTER TWENTY-SIX

CLARA

I'd hoped not to have to see Luke at all when I arrived at the hospital. Our schedules only overlapped by four hours, and ordinarily we were lucky to even see each other in passing. As luck would have it, as soon as I finished my rounds, I stepped out of the last room and saw his dark, curly locks bobbing as he spoke enthusiastically with one of the nurses.

I tucked my chin into my chest, rage bubbling in my stomach, and pushed myself forward.

Don't notice me.

Don't notice me.

Don't noti—

"Hey there, stranger. You avoiding me?" he teased, no idea he'd hit the nail on the head. I spun around, grimacing. Should I try to pretend everything was okay? This wasn't the time or place for a meltdown. I still had ten hours left in my shift.

"Nope. Just busy. I have surgery in thirty," I told him, glancing at my watch. "See you later."

His jaw dropped open slightly, and when I began to walk away, I heard his footsteps approaching me from behind. "I'm sorry I had to duck out early this morning. I had a few errands I had to run before work."

"It's fine."

"And then I had to go by and check on Naomi, let her know I wouldn't be home tonight. I plan on staying with you...if that's still okay?"

I stiffened at her name, but he obviously didn't notice. "I don't know. I may have to work late."

"I'll wait up for you."

"You should probably just go home, Luke," I said, shaking my head. I did not want to cry there. More than anything I'd ever wanted in my life, I did not want to cry in the hallway of my place of work over a man who'd lied to me. I deserved better. I'd worked so hard for better. I'd burned down my old life, left my deadbeat ex, created a whole new career for myself, worked my butt off to get every scholarship and every cent of aid I could, worked three jobs to pay off the rest, and now, here I was...standing in a hallway with tears in my eyes, my heart practically ripped out of my chest as I stared at a man I thought I knew.

He watched me crying, his expression changing from confusion to concern. "Clara, what is it?" he asked, lowering his voice slightly. He put a hand on my arm, looking over his shoulder. "What's wrong?"

I rubbed my lips together and swiped away my tears, though they continued to fall. "I can't do this right now. I have surgery."

"Not for half an hour," he said firmly. "You need to talk to me. Did something happen? Is it a patient?"

I could've lied—probably should've—but I didn't have it in me. I was exhausted and desperate for answers. Nodding my head toward the door to our right, I led the way toward the storage room and shut it behind me. I spun around, staring at him in the dim light of the room. He studied me carefully, unaware of the bombshell I was about to drop.

Welcome to the club.

"I need you to tell me the truth about Naomi."

Fear flickered across his expression, but he recovered quickly, pretending not to understand what I was asking. "What about her?"

"I went by your house this morning, Luke. I wanted to—"

"You did *what?*"

"You're married?" I demanded. "You're... God, Luke, *you're married?* How could you do this to me? How could you lie to me for this long?"

For a moment, I thought he was going to defend himself, to try and lie his way out of it, but quickly thereafter, his intense demeanor softened and his shoulders fell, as if they'd been relieved of a great weight, and he placed his face in his palms. "I'm so sorry, Clara. I... God, there's not even a good excuse. I know that. I never intended to lie." His face left his hands, and he met my eyes. "I swear to you, I didn't. When we met, I had no intention of lying to you. When I started falling for you, it was just the two of us. Honestly. I didn't even know Naomi at the time. We'd gone to college together, but we were never even friends then. I didn't know her... I still don't know her like I know you." He seemed as though he wanted to reach for me, but he didn't. "Naomi and I started seeing each other about six years ago. It was during that time when you thought the chief was giving you worse surgeries because he'd found out about us. You insisted we cool off for a while and I hardly saw you for six months... Do you remember?"

I didn't nod, though I did remember, of course. Was he honestly suggesting this was all my fault?

"Anyway, I met Naomi and saw her a few times casually, but then when you and I got back together, I stopped calling her. We never really defined what we had, so I didn't think it was a big deal." His chest rose with a heavy breath. "Then she told me she was pregnant. I couldn't just abandon her. I was drowning in debt, and I couldn't afford to be served with child support, too. So, I agreed to give it a try with Naomi. Not because I loved her, but because it was what I had to do."

"So why not tell me then, Luke? Why not spare me years of being lied to?"

"Because I love you," he said forcefully. "I love you more than I've ever loved anyone, Clara. You're the person who knows me best in all of the world. The person who understands me." He reached for my hand, but I jerked it away. "You must hate me. I don't blame you, but I swear to you, if I'd told you the truth all those years ago, there was a risk you would've walked away, and I couldn't stomach that."

"So you chose to lie to me? To lead me on? To promise me a future you could never give me?" I threw my arms down at my sides, realizing what this meant. Every promise he'd given me about our future was a lie. Every time he'd told me he wanted to live with me, he wasn't serious. I'd been all in, my heart was squarely in his hands, and he'd abused it.

"I was never leading you on—"

"You're *married*, Luke. What future could we possibly have? You told me she was crazy. That she was a danger to Becca. You told me that was why I could never meet her, because she was so fragile." My shaking fingers moved to cover my lips. "It was all a lie. Every single word for the last...what, six years?"

"None of it was a lie. Don't you see that? Not that I loved you. Not that I wanted to spend my life with you. I married Naomi out of duty, but we've never been together in the way you and I are. That ended so long ago between us. You're the woman I love. The woman I want a life with."

"Even if that's true, we can never have a life together, Luke. And, even if you left Naomi, even if you managed to free yourself up for me, I could never bring myself to trust you again. You lied about your wife's mental state to suit your situation. Do you have any idea how wrong that is?"

"I didn't lie!" he shouted, then lowered his voice. "Sorry. I just...I didn't. I mean, maybe Naomi isn't as bad off as I described her, but when she and I met, she was very depressed. Borderline suicidal. And the pregnancy was hard on her. She had so many health issues, and after Becca, she had such bad postpartum depression, I had to send her to a facility. I was going it completely alone for so long. Trying to balance my career, my relationship

with you, raising a newborn, keeping my house put together. She's better now—her medication is closely monitored, but she's doing better. After everything, I still can't bring myself to trust her completely."

"I can't listen to this," I said, shaking my head. "Regardless of what Naomi did or didn't do, has or hasn't done, she's your wife. You're married to her and you have an obligation to her. And to your child. You were right in thinking I would've left you if I'd known the truth all those years ago. You've wasted my time, Luke. You've wasted my time, which is dwindling anyway, and you've broken my heart. I don't know if I can ever forgive you for what you've done."

"You don't mean that…" His chin quivered.

"I do," I said, pressing my lips together. "I really, really do. I need you to give me some space. I need to process." I stepped back, a hand over my stomach as I willed myself not to be sick. I reached for the door, then froze and looked back over my shoulder. "You need to tell Naomi the truth."

With that, I disappeared through the door. I wasn't sure if it was a threat, if he'd assume I would tell Naomi if he didn't. I wasn't sure what I wanted to do. There were too many options, too many questions swimming through my head, all cloaked in massive heartbreak.

I just needed space.

I needed a moment to breathe.

Thank God, I was headed for a surgery. What I needed more than anything else was to cut something. And, at that point, it was Luke or a patient.

CHAPTER TWENTY-SEVEN

ALAINA

The text came in around two in the morning the day after the doctor's appointment. I wanted to hold out much longer, to stay mad at him for a longer period of time, to have him come back to me groveling. I supposed a text would have to work.

I'm sorry about the way I acted earlier. Can I come over?

I sent back a simple **k.** in hopes that he'd realize I was still upset. He still had some work to do. I climbed out of bed and slipped into the shower, scrubbing the sweat from my skin. I ran sudsy hands over my tiny bump, hoping that someday he'd look at it and be filled with as much love as I was. We'd made that. We'd created something from nothing. Our love had created life.

I grabbed my razor, shaving quickly. As mad as I was at him, I couldn't deny how badly I wanted to be with him again. It was sickening. I should've hated him, but I couldn't. I craved his touch like some pregnant women craved food. I longed for his hands on my skin, for the way he smelled, for the way he looked at me. I could only hope that he'd realized the error of his ways, that he was coming to apologize and beg for my forgiveness. I rinsed the conditioner from my hair when I was done shaving and stepped out of the shower. I wiped away a dry spot on the foggy mirror and examined my body.

I ran a hand over the paint palette tattoo on my upper thigh, then up my belly and toward my swollen breasts. Lucas had commented recently on their doubling in size, seemingly impressed. Taking that note to heart, I threw on a silk teddy that left nothing to the imagination and ran a comb through my short hair. I removed my lip ring and brushed my teeth, flossing until my gums bled. I swiped on deodorant and lotion, then flipped off the light when I heard the knock on the door.

I hurried into the bedroom and toward the hall, listening as the door opened. When I saw him, I slowed my steps, trying to appear seductive rather than frazzled. Using the hand behind his back, he shut the door without breaking eye contact, a crooked grin on his face.

"Hey," he said, breathless. He blinked slowly, lazily, and I realized something might be wrong.

"Hey..." I stepped forward.

"Areweokay?" he blurted out, the words all strung together as he took another step and stumbled forward.

I stepped back, staring at him as reality hit me. "Are you drunk?"

He rubbed his palm over his face. "I'm not as think as you drunk I am," he teased, letting out an obnoxious laugh as he took another drunken step forward.

"I thought you were at work." Anger bubbled in my

belly, and I found myself filling with disgust. Had he really gotten drunk and then drove to me?

"Rough day," he said with a sigh, not bothering to explain. It's not like that was new. He rarely told me much about his day. Or his life, if we were being honest. He took another step toward me and reached out his arm. I let him grip mine, but I didn't budge from my spot.

"I can't believe you drove drunk. Do you have any idea how stupid that is?"

"I'm not that drunk, honestly." He wiggled his shoulders one at a time over and over in a wave-like motion. "I'm just a little *loosey-goosey...*"

"What are you doing here, Lucas? Why did you come?" I rubbed my fingers across my throbbing temple, feeling mortified. I'd had so much hope for our evening, but it was obvious he'd called me for one reason alone. He was going to use me. Like he had before. Maybe it was all he'd ever done.

"I wanted to see you," he said, trying to maintain a serious face, though it looked more painful than anything.

"Why?"

He stepped forward, and I remained still, letting him approach me. "Because...I'm an idiot. And I missed you. And I wanted to be sure you were okay after...well, after everything."

I pressed my lips together. "You really hurt me, Lucas."

He closed his eyes, his brow furrowing. "I know."

"You embarrassed me. You made me look and feel like an idiot...like you didn't—*don't*—care." I felt bitter, betraying tears coming on.

"I do care. I care *so much*." His hands wrapped gently around my arms.

"How can you when you seem to hardly be able to stand being around me? I don't understand what you want from me. Am I just a booty call? Or just someone to make you feel less lonely?" When the tears began to fall, I refused to stop them or brush them away. I let him see what he was doing to me.

"How can you even ask that?" He leaned his head onto my shoulder. "I love you, Alaina. You've never been…*that* to me. You've always meant something."

"But you mean *every*thing to me, Lucas. Don't you see that? It isn't even. It isn't fair. And you come here like this, and I'm—God, I'm so stupid. I thought—I don't know what I thought. But I didn't want this. This conversation while you're drunk, when you won't remember half of what you're saying right now tomorro—"

He shoved his lips to mine, causing me to jump back, but his grip was tight on my arms. I gave in with a sigh, our lips barely parting. His hand moved to the back of my neck, the other on my waist as he pushed his mouth onto mine harder. His kiss tasted of bourbon and salt. His hands were hot on my skin, and though the anger I felt didn't dissipate totally, my hormones had control over my reaction. I leaned my head back as his lips left mine, trailing across my jaw bone and onto my shoulder blade. He brushed my gown off my shoulder in a second, pressing his lips to my flaming skin.

He cupped my breasts as his kisses trailed between them, pushing my gown the rest of the way to the floor. He stepped back, looking me over, his eyes dark with desire, then he licked his lips and scooped me up. He took heavy, loud steps down the hallway, trying to continue our kiss as we went. He stumbled, one hand gripping my waist and the other on the wall, as we neared the bedroom. Standing me back down on the ground, he separated his lips from mine as we made our way toward the bed. Then I let him lay me down, my hands lifting his shirt over his head and unbuttoning his pants. He reached for my hand, pulling me toward him, but I stopped, shaking my head.

"Come here," I whispered, wiggling a finger at him. I didn't want it to be rough, hot, and heavy like usual. I wanted it to be tender now. I wanted to feel the love between us. I wanted him to take care of me like he'd never done before.

He seemed confused, but bent his arm, leaning down beside me on the bed. He moved closer to me, his hand running through my hair as his tongue explored my mouth. He expelled a groan, rocking his hips against mine as he rolled over onto his back, leaving me beside him.

He glanced down, raising his brows in a way he so often did, his eyes darkening as he used the hand still in my hair to push my head in the general direction he wanted it to go. *Down.*

I pushed back. "I want to go slow. Enjoy it. I want you to take care of me first," I told him, moving his free hand between my legs.

He hesitated, removing his opposite hand from my hair. "Can I...I mean, can you... I thought—" He cut himself off, chewing on his bottom lip. "I didn't think you'd be able to."

"What do you mean?"

"Because...well, you know—"

"You know the doctor said sex is totally safe for the baby," I told him, trailing a finger across his chest. His hand lifted to mine in an instant, stopping the motion.

"The baby?" he demanded. I cocked my head to the side, confused as ever. "I thought you'd, er, well... You're still pregnant?"

Shock radiated through me, and I backed away from him on instinct, unable to stand my skin touching his. "Of course I'm still pregnant." My forehead wrinkled with fury. "You can't seriously think I'd have had an abortion already? You only suggested it yesterday!"

"I thought you would've had it taken care of when you were already at the hospital," he said, playing with the comforter awkwardly.

"It's not a bit of shopping, Lucas. I couldn't just take care of our child while I'm out! I don't even know that I want an abortion... You thought I'd want to have sex with you after just having our child aborted? *What's wrong with you?*" I stood from the bed, backing away from him in outright horror. "You...that's why you're here, isn't it? You thought this was all taken care of. You thought I'd just go out and do exactly as you'd asked without a care in the world or thought of my own. Is that really what you think of me? That I have no opinions?" I scowled, tearing open a drawer from behind me and pulling on shorts and a T-shirt.

He sat up, standing from the end of the bed and attempting to approach me, though I shoved him away. "Of course that's not what I think—"

"That's all I've ever showed you, isn't it? Every time we've eaten out, you've been the one to pick. Every time we've had a date, you've chosen where. When we hang out, you choose the day and time. I've followed your lead like a lost puppy dog." I put a hand on my stomach, staring into space as the reality crashed into me. "That's all you've known with me." I shook my head, watching as he lifted his pants from the ground. "I'm sorry, Lucas. I'm sorry for not showing you who I really am. I'm sorry I was so busy trying to impress you, to prove I was *worthy* of you, that I never let you see the real me. I am not a woman who bends to a man's will. I am not going to let you make a decision this huge for me. I..." I put a hand to my throat. "I can't breathe. Lucas, I can't...I ca—"

His eyes widened as he rushed toward me, my vision tunneling as I fought to take a breath. My heart thundered in my chest, the room beginning to spin as I pressed my back against the wall and slid down.

"Alaina?" he called, his arms around me as he helped me to the ground. He was saying something else, though his words sounded as if they were coming from underwater.

My breaths were coming quicker and more labored.

I felt a cool sweat gathering at my temples.

His hands were on me, holding me up...or maybe down.

I was falling or floating...

Nothing felt right.

He was blurry, then dark.

My head hit something hard.

Everything disappeared.

CHAPTER TWENTY-EIGHT

NAOMI

I walked through the foyer and living room with a pounding head, my arms wrapped tightly around me as it seemed the cool air of fall had finally arrived. I stopped short when I saw the muscled shoulders standing at the kitchen sink waiting for me, forgetting for just that split second about our guest.

"Sleep well?" I asked, my voice cracking with sleep.

Brent turned around, suds up to the middle of his arms, and shut off the water. "Sorry, did I wake you?"

"Not at all. I'm an early riser. It's basically my only alone time."

His expression fell. "And I'm interrupting that."

"No, of course not," I assured him. "And if interrupting anything means cleaning my house, I'd never complain." I smirked.

He shook his head. "I needed to keep my hands busy, and it's too early to head to the shop."

I walked toward the coffee pot, filling my faded green mug with fresh coffee. "Thank you, for this."

"I know you can't live without it." I knew he was feeling every bit as awkward as I was, try as he might to hide it. He leaned against the counter, drying his hands. "How'd you sleep?"

"I don't think you ever answered when I asked that question," I pointed out.

"Fair enough, but I think you already know the answer."

I took a sip of my coffee. "Was the couch uncomfortable?"

"The couch was fine," he said graciously. "The least of my concerns, to be frank."

"Lucas never came home," I told him.

"I noticed. Did you hear from him?"

"No. Not that that's unusual." His lip twitched with unspoken words, but he didn't speak. "Why didn't he tell me he was in contact with your mother? I thought neither of you had spoken to her in years."

He shook his head, moving to the coffee pot and filling a mug of his own. "Truth be told, I never have any idea why my brother does what he does, but especially not this. Last I heard, she was in South Dakota, with some man she met online." He took a sip and rolled his eyes, letting out a loud breath. "Probably bled him dry and moved home." He scoffed. "If she can even call this place home—we never stayed anywhere long enough to matter. As for why Lucas is helping her, I have no idea. She was just as bad to him as she was to me, maybe worse." His lips pressed into a thin line, muscles tensing in his shoulders and neck. "She doesn't deserve his help, Naomi. Definitely not his money."

"Maybe he doesn't know?" I offered. "Do you think maybe she got a hold of our banking information and put it in his name without him knowing?"

He didn't seem convinced, but he didn't answer right away. "You'd have to ask him." He resorted to grunting in between sips of coffee.

I watched him with fascination. I knew so little about my husband's family. Brent was the only connection, and we saw him so rarely, only when I made a point to invite him to dinners, holidays, and family events. But his mother—I'd resigned myself to never meeting her. "How bad was she?" I asked softly, regretting it the instant the question left my lips. "Your mom."

He glanced at me, his intense gray eyes drilling into mine. His face was stern, as if all the happiness had been sucked from his body. "There's not even a word for it, Naomi. I can't—" He slapped his palm on the counter. "I can't think of a single word that would describe the horror she put us through as kids."

I shivered at the thought. "I'm sorr—"

"Don't," he said stiffly. "You don't have to apologize for what she did to us. I don't need it."

His tone was abrasive, more so than I'd ever heard from him. "I'm—"

"She was a shit mom, okay?" he said, no real question in his tone. He rolled his eyes, his hand moving to his forehead. "The word mom isn't even a title she deserves. She birthed us. That's it. We did the rest."

I nodded, chewing on my bottom lip. "I know Lucas has said she was an addict."

"Was. *Is*, I'm sure. She was on everything you could

think of when we were kids. We bounced around from house to house, boyfriend to dealer. We never knew who either of our dads were, though I'm sure they aren't the same. The men she was with treated us like shit, some better than others, but none of them good. We were just in the way. The things we saw..." His upper lip curled. "We walked in on them shooting up, fucking, fighting... Whatever it was, we were right in the middle of it."

"That's terrible," I said, a lump in my throat preventing me from saying more. After a moment, I added, "I'm not sure how you survived it."

He ran a hand through his hair, looking away from me. "Truth be told, I'm not either. There was never any food in the house. Hardly ever had running water or electricity. Every once in a while, we'd end up in a house with other kids... Those were the best." He grimaced.

"Lucas never mentioned any other kids growing up..."

"Some of them he'd be too young to remember, and some of them just didn't last long." He sucked in a breath through his teeth. "Hell, maybe he's just lucky enough to have blocked most of it out. Our mom is a horrible human being. And our life... It wasn't good, Naomi. I don't know how else to describe it. It was just...that was the hand we were dealt. She never wanted any better for us. That was her choice. The needle over her children— always. If she could've, I'm sure she would've traded us for drugs a time or two." He shuddered, his hands closing into fists in front of him, arms drawn in close to his chest.

"Why didn't anyone help you? The school or...or friends...surely someone knew what was happening."

He pressed his lips together, the muscles in his shoulders tense. "Everyone knew. The school. Our bus drivers. The owners of the shops we'd try to steal from. No one cared enough to get involved. People don't really do that... There was one neighbor once. I think he took pity on us. He used to let Lucas and me come over to his garden and pick any vegetables we wanted. We'd spend... God, we'd spend hours over there, picking apples off his trees, tomatoes and cucumbers straight off the vine. It was the most food we'd ever been allowed to eat at once. I'm convinced he's the one who called social services on Mom, but he'd never admit it." He laughed dryly under his breath. "He probably saved our lives."

"So you went into foster care? Lucas has told me about that part...a little bit, anyway. How old were you?" I asked.

He ran a hand over his mouth. "Too old for it to have mattered in the long run. I was sixteen at the time. Lucas was twelve. No one wants teenagers. We bounced around from house to house for the next two years until I aged out and was able to take custody of him."

I could see the haunted look in his eyes, and I wondered if I was wearing something similar. "You saved his life, Brent. I can't understand why you hate each other so much."

"I got him out because I felt like I had to. It wasn't his fault that we grew up like we did. But that was where my obligation ended. He chose to be the person he is, to live the life he does. He could've had it all, Naomi. He got a scholarship for his first two years of college because he's always had a good pitching arm, but he lost that because of his grades, took out loans for the rest of it, and...well, you know the rest." He sighed. "I'm not proud of who he's

175

become. But whatever good he has done, whatever good he has in him, Martina had nothing to do with it. She doesn't deserve the acknowledgment of even still being alive. I had no idea if she was, truth be told. I don't know why Lucas is still in contact with her, or why he would have anything to do with her. He's old enough to remember all she put us through." He raised his eyes to glance at me, his expression haunted. "If she's around, Naomi, it can't be a good thing. She only brings trouble."

I stared at him in horror, a mixture of grief and disgust filling my stomach. "I can't even—"

"You don't have to say anything. It's done. I've moved on...and I thought Lucas had, too."

I put a hand on his arm, taking a half-step closer. "I don't have to say anything, I know, but I want to. I'm sorry you went through what you did. No one deserves a childhood like that."

He looked uncomfortable but didn't shy away from my touch. Instead, he kept his eyes locked with mine, staring in silence.

"I can't understand why he would keep this from me," I said eventually, breaking the tension and stepping back.

He blinked, coming out of a trance, and chewed his thumbnail. "I can't either, but I don't put anything past my brother anymore."

"What should I do?"

"What do you want to do?" he pressed, pushing himself away from the counter so he was standing straight in front of me.

"If he knew about this, maybe even if he didn't, I think I want to leave him," I admitted, a truth I'd kept quiet, even from myself, for so long. "The way he's been lately... the things he's said. It isn't what I want anymore. But I'm scared."

"Scared of him?"

"Scared of losing Becca. We had a fight, and he threatened to take her from me."

"He's out of his mind," he scoffed. "No judge worth his salt would—"

"Take a child from a mother who suffers from chronic depression?"

He swallowed, obviously unaware of my diagnosis. Lucas hadn't told him. His eyes danced between mine. "I know I shouldn't worry about it. It's common, and I have it under control now. My doctor manages my medication, and I've learned coping mechanisms. I do therapy. I'm doing everything I can to make sure I'm healthy enough to raise Becca, but Lucas could still use it against me in court. He was so convincing when he threatened it... I can't help but worry."

"Lucas is the picture of good mental health?" he asked, raising a brow.

"I can't lose her, Brent. She's...she's everything to me."

He shook his head, and it was his turn to reach out, his fingers brushing the skin on my arms. "You aren't going to lose her. We won't let that happen. You may have your issues, Naomi, but you're a damn good mother. Take it from someone who knows what a bad one is. That little girl is loved and taken care of. Any judge worth a damn could see that."

I smiled with one side of my mouth, glancing down where our bare feet were just inches from each other's on the cherry floor. "He'll try to take her from me. He's already said. If I serve him with papers, it'll be a fight. Even if I win, how can I put her through that? Always having to choose sides? Always seeing us fighting?"

He pressed his lips together, studying my expression. "Having a happy home doesn't mean having people pretending to be happy. As she gets older, do you really want her to think what you two have is the picture of happiness she should strive for? Is this the kind of marriage you want for her?" When I didn't answer, he went on. "What do you want for her, Naomi? In life? In a partner? What do you want for your daughter?"

I jolted, forcing the answer out as his questions continued. "I want her to be happy. I want her to feel loved. Appreciated. Taken care of."

He closed his eyes slowly, and when he opened them, there was an emotion I didn't recognize on his face. "So why do you deserve any less?"

"You don't think Lucas loves me?"

"Shouldn't you be able to adamantly argue that he does?"

"I know he does—"

"My brother isn't capable of loving anyone but himself. Not really. He never has been. He's just like my mother. They both use people until they're of no further use to them, and then they cut their losses and disappear. For my mother, it was to get drugs. For Lucas it's, I don't know, it's to feel good about himself, I guess. To prove that he's worthy of love, even if he won't give it in return. He uses and manipulates. It's what he's always done. Girl-friends, friends, me... Lucas isn't capable of caring about anyone. Or experiencing happiness. Or feelings of any kind, for that matter. He only wants what brings him pleasure in the moment. As soon as he's done with you, as soon as you are no longer of any use to him, he'll cut you off—whatever that means for your relationship."

"What are you talking about? That's not true. He loves me. He *loves Becca*."

"He knows how he's supposed to feel about you both, sure. He knows how he's supposed to react and what he's supposed to say. He watches people, imitates what he sees, but Lucas isn't capable of loving anyone—not like you or me."

I furrowed my brow at him. "Why are you telling me this now?"

"Because he's back talking to my mom, maybe he never stopped, but if he's around her, his behavior is sure to get worse. And because I thought you were happy with him... I've never wanted to disrupt that, but I'm seeing now that you aren't. At least not in the way that you used to be. If you're planning to leave him, I want you to know what you're dealing with. I want you to know he's not going to make any decisions out of empathy or love. His desires are purely selfish—he wants to win, he wants to be in control, he wants to have the power. Losing you... losing Becca, those things won't help him accomplish any of his goals." He swallowed, taking another drink of his coffee. "He could be dangerous, Naomi. I don't want you to get hurt."

His words struck me, like bricks to the chest. "No... I mean, Lucas would never... He's not violent. He wouldn't *hurt* us."

He didn't seem convinced as he drained the mug, setting it on the counter with finality. "I just want you to promise me you'll be smart. Pick a day when he's out of the house, and you and Becca should leave. You can tell him it's happening once you're somewhere safe."

I swallowed. "You're...serious about this, aren't you?"

His eyes were stone as he reached out, taking my arms in his hands. "Deadly."

"You're scaring me..." I told him, trying to stop the shaking that had become evident in his arms. He trailed a finger across my shoulder and stopped just under my jaw.

"I'd never let anything happen to you. Either of you. You know that, right?" I tried to nod, but a tear slipped out, giving away my lie. He used his thumb to brush it away, his concerned eyes drilling into mine. "You're safe with me, Naomi. You always have been."

"Why are you so good to me?" I whispered, a tear dripping from my top lip.

His eyes softened even more, the answer there in the sterling gray tone of his irises. "Because, unlike my brother, I do know how to love."

I sucked in a sharp breath as I watched his lips lower toward mine. I should've stopped it. Should've said no, backed away. But just like the last time, I remained frozen, simultaneously wanting it to stop and never wanting it to end. His lips met mine with passion, and I melted into his arms, forgetting, just for the moment, all the darkness just over the horizon.

CHAPTER TWENTY-NINE

CLARA

"What do you mean you told Naomi?" I called into the phone, sidestepping out of the congested hospital hallway and against a wall between patient rooms.

"I told her everything. She wants me to leave. She's going to give me the divorce." His voice was breathless, like he'd been running. "Did you mean it when you said you'd leave with me if I wanted you to?"

"I—" I froze, the question catching me off guard. "I don't know, Luke. I said that before you lied to me. I don't know how to feel about everything right now. I don't know how you can expect me to answer something like that right now." I glanced behind me in the hallway. "I just need time to think. We should discuss this more. Where are you?"

"I'm leaving Naomi's now. I've packed a bag. I'm...I'm leaving town, Clara, and I'm not coming back. Are you coming with me, or aren't you?"

My heart picked up speed, my body ice cold. "What do you mean you're leaving town? Right now?"

"I can't be here anymore. It's too hard. Naomi wants us to have our space and her family is here, so it's only fair that I be the one to leave. Only..." He paused. "Only I don't want to leave without you." His voice was filled with whimsy as he spoke. "We can go anywhere you want. Hot, cold, north, south. Tropical. Snowy. Wherever you want to go, just name the place and we'll go there. We'll start our lives together. Get a place. Get jobs. Just...just be together. Isn't that what we've always wanted?"

I lowered my voice. "It-it is. Yes, of course, but...I mean, I thought we could plan it, though. I mean we have jobs here. Good jobs. Do you really want to leave with no notice? And, more than that, I have an apartment, a lease. We have commitments here, friends. We aren't teenagers, Luke. We can't just pack up and move and hope no one notices. There are things we have to take care of."

"We can take care of all that from wherever we are. We'll tell the hospital there's been an emergency and we're having to relocate. Your lease only has about four months left on it, so we can pay it up and sell your things." He sighed. "I just thought we could do this together...something freeing and exciting and new. I thought we could be kids again, Clara. That's how you make me feel, like a stupid teenager in love for the very first time." He chuckled. "I don't know what to do with my feelings for you."

I felt heat rush to my face, placing a hand over my cheek. "I—"

"Just withdrawal," I heard him whisper.

"Sorry?"

"Sorry, I'm just at the bank," he said, then I heard a shuffle as his palm swiped across the microphone. "What do you mean?" A pause. "No, that's impossible. Check it again."

"Luke, what's going on?"

He wasn't listening to me anymore, too busy arguing with the teller. "I don't care what it says. I know what's in there." Another pause, a hateful sigh. "Is there a manager I can speak to? Oh, of course she is."

"Luke, I should let you—"

"Yeah, no. Just…I'll be back." He growled, and I heard the microphone being swiped with skin again. "Sorry, you still there?"

"I'm here. Is everything okay?"

"When do you get off?"

"In about an hour. Is everything okay?" I repeated.

His tone lightened. "Everything's fine. Just a misunderstanding. I'll have to come back tomorrow morning when the manager's here. Can I meet you at home when you get off?"

Home. The word warmed me to my core. *Our* home. *Finally.* He was offering me all I'd ever wanted with him. Was I really going to deny how badly I wanted it?

I smiled to myself, rubbing my palm over my eyes. "Yeah, I'll be there around seven."

I could hear the smile in his voice when he responded. "I'll be waiting."

183

When I arrived home that evening, Lucas was waiting on the porch, a beer in his hand. I walked up the steps to the apartment, entering through the side door and walking through the apartment to meet him on the porch.

When I opened the door, he turned his head, appearing shocked to see me. His expression warmed as his eyes met mine. There he was. The man I'd known. The man I'd loved. The man who'd come before the lies.

I still wasn't okay with what he'd done, try as I might to rationalize it, but the truth was, I'd come before Naomi. He'd married her out of duty. Because he was a good man. The lies didn't negate that. He'd done what he could to do right by us both.

I hated how much it hurt me. I hated that I'd been so naïve, but that hatred didn't erase the love I felt for him. It didn't take away the twelve years of memories we'd made.

I fell into his arms, the fight becoming a silent memory that I feared would forever sit between us. I loved him. I was angry with him. I was hurt. I was happy. I wanted to be with him. I finally could. Finally, the invisible wall between us had been removed. Finally, I could have him in every way.

I looked up at him, my vision blurring with tears, and his expression said he knew my every thought. I was sure he did. Luke knew me. He always had. I smiled at him, my chin quivering, and he placed a finger under my chin, lifting his lips to mine.

"I love you," he whispered, seconds before he pressed our lips together.

I couldn't say it back, but I didn't need to. He felt it in

the way I held him, in the soft exhale from my lips. I didn't need to say anything with Luke. He'd always just known.

When we broke apart, he pulled me to his chest, rubbing my back, kissing my hair. "I'm so sorry, Clara. I'm an idiot."

"You are," I agreed, looking up at him and pressing myself up on my tiptoes to kiss him again. "But I love you anyway."

"Have you thought any more about my offer?"

"To run away together, you mean?" I teased. "That offer?"

"That offer," he confirmed, one brow raised as he waited for me to answer. As if there was any choice.

I chewed my lip, making him think I was considering it. "When will we leave?"

"You mean you'll go?"

"I wish you were less impulsive," I admitted, "and that I had time to actually plan for this, but I'd be lying if I said I thought I could let you leave and dismiss the chance to go with you. I need to be with you, Luke. Here, there, wherever you go. I love you. I want to be with you in whatever capacity I can 'til the end of time." I stepped back, pressing a finger into his chest. "On one condition…"

A broad grin grew on his face, though he hesitated slightly. "What's that?"

"No more lies. No more secrets."

He cocked his head to the side, and his shoulders tensed. If I hadn't known him so well, I would've believed him. Instead, I watched the telltale signs happen before my eyes. "No more lies, my love. No more secrets. I want you to know everything about me."

I only knew one thing as he spoke the words, one thing he'd never fool me about again: he was still lying. About what, I wasn't sure. But I couldn't let myself be deceived again.

CHAPTER THIRTY

ALAINA

W hen I came to, I was alone. The room was dark, my memory foggy. I tried to sit up in bed, though my body was rigid and sore. As I sat up, the cover fell away, and I realized I was still dressed in my T-shirt and shorts, my clothing soaked in sweat. There was a sliver of light peeking through the curtains to my right, a sign that it was morning and I was home. I reached over, flicking on the lamp on my bedside table and glancing around.

What had happened? I tried to recall my last memories.

The texts.

Lucas was drinking.

The fight.

He'd wanted me to have an abortion.

The fight.

The tunneling vision.

The tight chest.

Lucas' arms around me.

Lucas.

I listened carefully, through the quiet apartment, trying to determine if I was alone. There were no discernible noises. I glanced back at the nightstand again, trying to clear the sleep from my eyes. There was a glass of water on the nightstand next to a scrawled note in handwriting I recognized at once.

I picked up the note first, reading over it.

You had a panic attack from stress...I gave you some medicine to calm you. You may feel a little weak. Just stay in bed today. I'll be back after work to check on you. Love you.

I picked up the glass of water, noticing, just as he'd said, how weak I felt. The glass shook in my hand as I lifted the room temperature water to my lips. I took a sip before picking up my phone.

A whole day had passed, I realized, my head pounding. How was that possible?

I checked Facebook and Instagram, replying to a few emails about my paintings, then closed my eyes. I had a headache, and the scrolling of my phone wasn't helping. Something just didn't feel right.

I went to my recent calls. As much as I didn't want to be around Lucas at that moment, he was a doctor. He was the only person I could trust to take care of me.

The phone rang five times and, just when I was sure it was going to go to his voicemail, I heard him come on the line, his voice low.

"Hello?"

"Lucas? Where are you?"

"What's wrong?" he asked, his voice higher than usual.

"Nothing's wrong. I just…I don't feel well."

"Your anxiety caused a panic attack early yesterday morning, do you remember? I gave you a mild sedative to calm you down—"

"A mild—"

"It won't hurt the baby, don't worry. It's not much stronger than acetaminophen. Just enough to knock the edge off and help you sleep."

"Can you come take care of me? I don't want to be alone."

"I'll come over in a few hours, okay? I have a few things to take care of first."

I sighed, my stomach growling. "I'm hungry."

"I'll pick you up some food. You should really just be resting."

"I have a headache," I whined.

"It's normal. I came by this morning to check on you, but you were still out of it. There's a Tylenol in your drawer just in case it gets worse. Take it if you need to. You're probably thirsty. Don't let yourself get dehydrated… Did you drink the water I left you?"

I eyed the water, my body chilling at something in his tone. "Yes," I lied.

"Good. Just rest then, okay? Everything's going to be okay." There was relief in his words that had my heart pounding.

I stood from the bed, forcing myself to move through the weakness. I walked to the bathroom, lifting the glass up to the light and staring at the fizz at the bottom of my glass. He'd dissolved something in my drink. I knew it in an instant. "I have to go…" I whispered, all power lost from my voice.

"Are you—"

I tossed the phone to the floor, dumping the water down the drain and falling to the floor, finger down my throat until I felt the vomit begin to rise. I emptied my stomach until there was nothing left in me.

Then, I passed out.

CHAPTER THIRTY-ONE

NAOMI

When the front door slammed open on the evening before my husband's death, I knew his mood immediately. Not by the quick slam, which was usual no matter his mood, but by the heavy footsteps that followed it. He headed my way instinctually, as if we were pulled together by magnets.

Brent looked up at me from across the table, wiping a napkin across his face to wipe away the beef au jus from the corner of his lips. He scooped up Becca without a word, seeming to know what was going to happen.

Lucas entered the kitchen, taking in the scene. Becca in Brent's arms, Brent standing from the seat that should've been my husband's. His eyes locked with mine, though Becca squealed for him. "Daddy's home!" she cried, holding her arms out for him.

"Hi, baby," he said, not bothering to make eye contact with her, his focus on me. "Can you take her out of here?" he asked, looking at Brent for half a second. Brent looked at me. I thought getting Becca out had been his plan all along, but in that moment, at Lucas' suggestion, he hesitated.

"I think I should stay," he said firmly.

"No, I don't think you should," Lucas snapped, his lips tight. Becca watched him closely, her expression changing as her eyes traveled between the two of us.

"I don't give a—"

"Brent—" I cut him off, a hand held in the air. "It's fine. Just...would you take Becca outside to play for a bit? Give us a minute?"

"I don't want to go!" Becca cried.

"I know, baby, but you should go play with Uncle Brent. I'll bet you can beat him at hide-and-seek. What do you think?" I asked, forcing a smile.

Brent left the room slowly, keeping his eyes trained on me, and for just that moment, I felt safe. As he disappeared, the room cooled quickly. The safe feeling disappeared.

"What the hell do you think you're doing?" Lucas demanded, taking a heated step toward me. I pushed back further from the table, standing up.

"What do you mean? He's visit—"

"Where did all our money go?" he asked, spittle forming in the corners of his mouth.

My heart dropped. He hadn't been meant to notice the withdrawal I'd made the day before. Had the bank called him? "What are you talking about, Lucas?"

"I'm talking about our checking account, our savings... they've both been emptied. What are you doing? Are you thinking of leaving me? Stealing from me?" He took another step toward me, and I moved an equal distance back, our magnets now polarized.

"Why were you checking our accounts?" I asked cautiously.

"I visited the bank today," he said smugly. "They said we only have twenty-five dollars left in either account... What have you done with the rest?"

I swallowed, considering lying, but it would do no good. I chose a hint of the truth instead. "I moved it all into Becca's trust." *The one with your name nowhere on it. The one she can't touch until she's eighteen.* "There were a few transactions in the checking that I didn't recognize. The bank thought it would be safer to close the accounts and open new ones altogether. I'm in the process of doing that."

He scowled. "What kind of transactions?"

"Rent payments," I said coolly. "For an apartment downtown. I received the address from the company, and I'll be turning it over to the police. I have an appointment to go to the station this afternoon. It looks like we were hacked." His expression went ashen.

"I..." He ran a hand over his face, and I could see the thoughts swirling in his dark eyes. "I didn't realize."

"You don't know anything about that, do you?"

He grimaced, a deep wrinkle forming on his forehead. "No, of course not. Why would I?"

"Well, the apartment was listed in your name."

He went pale, his jaw slack. "I...Naomi—"

"The bank said it could still be fraudulent, but I wanted to ask you before I talked to the police."

"Right," he said quickly. "Well, I'll have to think. I

mean, I don't remember renting an apartment… Why don't you let me handle talking to the police? I can talk to the apartment company first, see what's going on."

"You'd remember renting an apartment, surely."

He nodded. "Right, of course. Well, either way, I can take over handling this."

I waved him off, pretending to think the offer was gracious. "Oh, I don't think that'll be necessary. I'm sure you have work."

He shook his head all too quickly. "Nonsense. You shouldn't have to take Becca downtown to the police station. I can handle it on my way to work."

"That's why Brent's here. He's going to help me with her. I know how busy you are." My innocent act was careless, and I knew it shouldn't have fooled him, but he seemed too preoccupied trying not to get caught to realize he already had.

"You don't need my brother to help you. He shouldn't know our business," he snarled, the space between his eyes crinkling with frustration. Any sliver of civility was gone at the mention of his brother. "He shouldn't even be here. You should've told me about this and let me handle it."

"Oh, when?" I asked, slamming the chair into the table at the notion. "When exactly would you have liked for me to do that? When you were running out the door on your way to work, or storming out the door after telling me I was too crazy to take care of our daughter?" I walked around the back of the table, circling it to get out of the dining room. He moved to block the door, his stance set firm.

"That's what this is about, isn't it? We had a fight, and you thought you'd teach me a lesson by stealing from me?"

I let out a snort. "*Stealing* from you? Oh, really? We both know that's impossible." He grabbed my arm, and I jerked it away, shoving past him and through the doorway. "Between all your debt and student loans, there's nothing left to steal. There never has been. The money is mine, Lucas—"

"It's your parents' money," he argued, turning around and following me into the foyer with heavy footsteps. "You haven't done any interior design since Becca was born, and even before that, come on, Nae, it was a joke."

I spun around, shocked by the harshness of his words. "I cannot believe you just said that to me." I rested my hand on the railing of the stairs, half for comfort and half to keep me from falling over. Lucas had never spoken to me in such a way. Until Sunday, two days ago. That was when something in him seemed to have snapped. What was it? What changed?

"You stole from me!"

"I'm not stealing anything—"

"What do you call it, then?" he demanded. "You took money from our account without telling me."

"What did you need the money for anyway?" I asked, shaking my head. "You never get cash. The bills have already been paid for the month. Gas and food go on the AmEx. You should be set."

"I was…" His eyes darted back and forth, obviously trying to fabricate whatever he was about to tell me. "One of the nurse's kids is having a fundraiser at school. I was trying to help out… They get a bike or something if they hit their goal."

"You couldn't write a check?"

"Does it matter how I paid? Don't try to turn this around on me! You're the one hiding things!"

I scoffed, unable to hold it back any longer. "Oh, I am, am I?" I turned around on the stairs, stomping up them in a way that would've gotten Becca scolded.

"What's that supposed to mean?" He jogged after me.

I stopped so abruptly he shoved into me. I turned back around. "It's supposed to mean I don't think I'm the one with all the secrets, Lucas. I'm not the one hiding things and sneaking around."

He scowled. "What the hell are you talking about?"

"You know *exactly* what I'm talking about," I said, poking my forefinger into his chest. "I know the truth, Lucas. I know what you've been doing, and it's over."

His lips pressed together, but he didn't deny anything. "I'm leaving you, Naomi."

I let out a deep, throaty laugh, my hands clutched to my chest. "Oh, whatever will I do without you at night… oh wait. Well, what will I do without you during the day then…oh…wait. What about without your help parenting —" I tapped my finger onto my chin. "No, you don't do that either. Hmm… You know, I'm realizing, what is it you do for me in this marriage anyway?"

"You bitch!" he cried, stepping toward me menacingly.

I held my ground until our chests were mere centimeters apart. "Call me all the names you want, Lucas. Throw your tantrum, tell your lies. At the end of the day, I'm exhausted from caring. I can't make myself care anymore.

I want you out of the house. I don't care where you go. I don't care what you do. Just get out." I waved my hand in the air, gesturing toward the door. My heart thudded loudly in the silence, my face hot with anger.

A muscle in his jaw twitched as he stared at me. "I'll get custody of Becca."

The words hurt, but not like he'd hoped. It was a threat I had known was coming, but one that stung nonetheless. I held my ground. "Good luck with that...without any money." I let the words leave my mouth nice and slow, weighing each syllable on my tongue.

His hands balled into fists at his sides, his shoulders rising practically to reach his ears. "I will get half of that money. It's mine! I earned it being married to *you*."

"I guess that's up to the court to decide," I said with a shrug. "But we both know even if you get half of what was in our account, the money will run out. Mine won't. You mentioned my mental health, Lucas, but what about yours? I have the resources to get help with my issues. You never have. A childhood of neglect and abuse could be just as damaging as depression, and there's no pill for that." I clicked my tongue, feigning concern.

"You have no idea what I'm capable of," he said, taking another step toward me until our feet were intertwined on the same step. I leaned back, feeling the anger rising in my chest that I'd only just been able to keep at bay.

"No, dear husband. I think it's *you* who has no idea what *I'm* capable of. I can dig up every piece of dirt on you, hire private investigators, whatever it takes to prove you're an unfit father. Given your track record, I don't think it'll be that hard. If you push me on this, I will make sure you never see your daughter again. Never get a penny." His expression changed, grew colder. "But if you walk away, let this divorce go through like it should, you'll get what you deserve out of this marriage."

"I will get half," he said, leaning in so our foreheads were touching. He grabbed my arm, his fingers digging into my flesh.

"You deserve nothing," I argued. "Whatever I give you will be a gift." I jerked my arm out of his grasp. "And don't touch me."

He took a half-step back, one foot leaving the step we'd shared. "You're nothing but a spoiled little brat, Naomi. That's all you've ever been. Run back to Mommy and Daddy and let them fix the problem like always." He shoved a finger against my forehead, bouncing it away from him. "Too bad that can't fix that fucked up little brain of yours."

I swatted his finger away, my blood boiling as I matched his motion, putting my palm on his forehead. "At least my parents cared to try." I pushed back against his head, watching as it bobbed back as mine had, but never returned forward. Instead, his expression changed from anger to fear in a split second as his head continued falling back, followed by his shoulders. His arms twirled circles as he tried to catch his balance, and I threw my arms forward, reaching for his shirt.

He fell back in a second, though it seemed to happen in slow motion. His body crumpled as his back slammed into the stairs behind him, and he rolled down, feet over head, then on his side. I stood frozen in place, replaying my actions as I watched it happen.

What had I done?

I stared at the body at the bottom of the stairs in horror, my eyes filling with heavy tears. I took a cautious step down, then another. "Lucas?" I called quietly, picturing the police cars that would line the driveway, my face on the news. They'd take Becca away. I'd be thrown in jail.

It was an accident.

Did it matter?

As I neared the bottom step, he let out a groan, his body twitching to life. I choked back a sob, crouching down beside him as he stared around the room, appearing confused. When his eyes met mine, he startled, then pushed himself up and away from me.

Dark, crimson blood stained the white, marble floor at the foot of the stairs.

"You tried to kill me," he stammered, his voice thick with saliva, like he was fighting off a cold.

"Lucas, no— It was an accident... I didn't—"

He put a hand to the back of his head, wincing and pulling it back as he looked at his blood-soaked palm. "I'm so sorry—" I said through my tears. He stared at me in horror, then turned, stumbling as he walked away and toward the door.

"Let me take you to the hospital!" I yelled after him, trembling in place. I couldn't move, the fear closing in around my throat. At least he was alive, but did that make this any less of a crime?

He grumbled something under his breath, pulling open the door, one hand still on the back of his head and a trail of blood running down the back of his green scrubs.

He shut the door without looking back at me and, with his absence, I let myself collapse in the sobs I'd known were coming. I fell to the ground next to the blood on the floor, thick and dark like ink. I covered my mouth, closing my eyes and looking away.

When the door opened, I looked up, seeing the wrong brother staring back at me taking in the scene. Becca was just behind him, her tiny face peeking around his legs. It was then I noticed the smeared, bloody handprint on the wood of the door, and I knew what this must look like to them.

What have I done?

CHAPTER THIRTY-TWO

CLARA

The heavy footsteps coming down the hall roused me from my sleep. I rolled over, glancing at the time. It was just after two in the morning—earlier than I'd expected Luke to be getting home. I pulled the sheet up over my bare chest as I sat up when the bedroom door opened.

He didn't bother turning on the light as he entered the room. His shoulders were slumped, and he walked past the bed without a word.

"Good morning. You're home early," I called, though he didn't answer. "Luke?" He stopped in the bathroom doorway, looking back at me. I took in his silhouette, almost creepy in the dark room. "You okay?"

He grunted a quick, "Yes," while continuing to stare at me.

"Where have you been? Why'd you let me sleep so long?" I adjusted even more on the bed, watching him closely. Something was off, but I couldn't put my finger on what it was. Something had upset him.

"I had to run an errand," he said simply, then stepped into the bathroom. "Don't freak out." He offered the warning seconds before he flipped on the light, but I had no time to process or heed the words. The back of his head was coated with thick blood, his hair matted. The blood was dried on the back of his neck, down the back of his scrubs. I leapt from the bed, rushing across the room. "Oh my God, Luke. Your head! What happened?"

He winced as I touched it. "Naomi and I got into a fight."

"She did this to you?" I asked in horror, rubbing my hands carefully through his hair as I tried to find the wound. When I brushed my hands over a particularly stiff patch of hair, the blood began to ooze again.

"She told me she wanted me to come back, that she'd made a mistake telling me to leave, but I told her I was leaving her." His eyes met mine in the mirror over the sink. "For you. I don't want to try with her anymore. It's you I want."

I sucked in a breath, breaking eye contact to tend to the wound. "Luke, I can't—we have to get you to the hospital. You need stitches, a CT."

He shook his head, pulling away from me. "I don't want to get her into trouble. She was upset. With her *issues*...sometimes she can't control her temper."

I pressed my lips together, staring at the beautiful, self-less man in front of me. "She can't get away with this, Luke. She could've killed you."

"I don't want to hurt her any more than I have. I'm breaking her heart, ruining her life. I probably deserved this. And I'm fine, honestly. I just need you to sew it up."

He parted his hair with his fingers, giving me a cleaner view of the gash at the back of his skull. "So we can get going."

"Going? Where are we going?"

He gave a lopsided grin. "To start our new lives."

My chest constricted. "We're leaving today? You still want to do this?"

He scoffed. "Now more than ever."

"But is it safe to leave her with Becca? Should we wait until you can get custody?"

His expression darkened. "I can't wait, Clara. I have to get away from here. Away from *her*. I-I don't feel safe here."

A lump formed in my throat at the words, and I stared at him, watching as he removed one hand from the back of his head. The blood trickled through his stained fingers, the other making crimson fingerprints as he opened my drawers, rifling through them. When he found what he was looking for, he held it up. The black leather housed a suture kit I'd bought and never used.

"I need your help, Doctor," he said, the joke there in his voice, masked behind the pain.

I sighed, taking the kit from him. "Sit down." I gestured toward the toilet, and he put the lid down, taking a seat. I turned on the faucet, scrubbing my shaking hands. I'd done stitches a million times, but never on someone I loved. I scrubbed them with the soap until my fingers were raw, cleaning under my short fingernails, down the length of my forearm, and between my fingers. I lifted my hands like I was prepared for surgery. "Can you turn the water off?" He nodded and stood, while I turned my attention to the open suture kit on the side of the counter, pulling on the gloves. I spun around when I heard a loud buzz, my jaw dropping open. "What did you do?"

He stood in front of me, his beard trimmer in hand, a chunk of dark hair behind him on the floor. "You weren't going to be able to see the wound otherwise."

I shook my head, tutting under my breath. "I could've seen it fine. You didn't need to shave your head."

"It's just hair," he said, raising one shoulder in a shrug. "It'll grow back. It's what we tell our patients." With that, he laid the trimmer down and took a seat back on the toilet.

I tore open the blue pack of nylon sutures and laid them next to the needle holder. "I don't have anything to numb you."

He inhaled sharply through his teeth as I swiped the prep pad across the wound. "I can handle it."

I worked in silence, weaving the needle through his skin, more aware of my technique than ever before. He stayed eerily still, his hands grasping his knees and eyes squeezed closed, until I'd performed the last suture. I stared at my work with pride as I covered it in gauze. "There. How are you feeling?"

"Like someone's been sewing my skin," he said with a chuckle before standing. He leaned down and kissed my lips briefly. His skin smelled of cigarette smoke and, when he pulled away, I noticed his pupils were more dilated than usual. "Thank you. I promise I'll pay you back if we're ever in a reverse situation."

"Let's hope we aren't."

He gave a sly smile. "Let's hope we aren't," he repeated, making his way to the sink and washing his hands.

"Have you been smoking?" I followed him across the room.

"Of course not, why would you ask that?"

"You smell like it," I said firmly. "You don't smoke, Luke."

He sighed. "I stopped by my mom's apartment before I came here. To get something stronger for the pain."

I stared at him, so many questions swirling through my mind I wasn't sure which to ask first. "Your mom? You mean...you took drugs?"

"Relax. Just a few hydrocodone. Something to knock the edge off."

"That was really stupid, you know that? What if you'd gotten caught? You could lose your license." I paused, waiting for him to answer, but he didn't, studying his hands as he scrubbed. "Why would your mom have pain pills?"

"She's always got something..." He trailed off, and I pursed my lips, reality setting in. His phone buzzed in his pocket, and he pulled it out. The letter M lit up his screen, and he hit ignore, sliding it back in his pocket and grumbling, "Speak of the devil."

Chills lined my skin as it all sank in. "That was your mom calling? I was right, wasn't I? About your mom being an addict? I had it right the first time."

He sighed. "I forgot I'd told you, and once I was going on about Naomi's parents, I had to keep lying. I'm an idiot, and I'm sorry."

I sighed through my nose. "Yeah, you are. Luke, you

told me your mom was dangerous. You hadn't spoken to her in years."

"Yeah, that part wasn't a lie. I hadn't in a long time. She's come back within the last few years. She's in a rough spot, and she's needed my help. She's trying to get clean, and I'm in a place where I can help her. What kind of son would I be if I said no?"

I ran a hand through my hair as I tried to take in all that he was saying. "I know you're trying to do the right thing, but it doesn't sound like she's trying to get clean if she had pills on hand to give you." He frowned, and I went on, "I just don't want you to get hurt…"

"I know—"

"You shouldn't be going around her when she's using, and you certainly shouldn't be taking drugs from her—"

"I know," he said more firmly. "You asked me not to lie to you anymore, and I'm not. Isn't that a good thing?"

I pressed my lips together. "Yes, I guess so."

"Good. And I won't be seeing her anymore. I just went by to tell her I was leaving."

"You wha—"

"Now," he interrupted when he was done drying his hands, "get your bag packed. I'll be back in a few hours, and we'll hit the road."

"Hang on. Where do you think you're going?" I asked, putting a hand to his arm. "You've just had a major head injury. You need to rest. I should be monitoring you for a few hours."

He laughed, brushing off my touch. "I'm fine, honestly. I've had worse, trust me. I'm a bleeder, always have been. I just have a few things to take care of before we hit the road."

"You can't drive in your condition!"

"I drove over here, didn't I? I only ran over two puppies." He snorted, patting my head. "I'm fine. Swear." He turned away dismissively, preparing to leave the bathroom, but I moved in front of him with one hand on my hip.

"What do you have to take care of that's so important? At least let me drive you."

"Don't worry," he said, "I have no intentions of dying before I get to make you my wife."

My chest swelled, head pounding at the words. "What are you talking about?"

He twisted his mouth. "You've gone and made me ruin the surprise now."

"You said you didn't want to get married."

"Because I already was... Soon enough that won't be an issue. I was going to pick up your ring before the trip." He paused, his smile slight. "Is that okay with you?"

I couldn't deny the happiness radiating from me. It was all I'd ever wanted. I leapt forward, throwing my arms around him. "Oh, Luke..."

"Watch the head," he said, jerking down as my hands swung around his neck. He laughed and kissed me back, his hands on my waist. "I love you."

"I love you, too..." I told him, watching in a dream-like stupor as he walked past me, with one last look back, out of the bedroom and down the hall. A few moments later, I heard the door shut, snapping me out of my trance.

Oh, no.

Proposal or no, I couldn't let him drive away. Not in his condition. Not with a head wound and on whatever he'd taken. I grabbed my clothes from the edge of the bed, throwing them over my head as quickly as I could manage. Then, I grabbed the keys and rushed out the door, not bothering to lock it behind me. I didn't have time.

I had to save a life.

CHAPTER THIRTY-THREE

ALAINA

He opened the door and entered my apartment in one fluid movement. I was on the couch in sweats and a T-shirt, my hair slicked back from my face with a cloth headband.

When he entered, I tried to sit up, but fell back down, feigning weakness.

"I'm sorry I couldn't get here sooner." He looked me over. "What's wrong?" When he moved closer, I realized there was blood on the collar of his scrubs. "What happened?"

"I should ask you the same thing," I said, lifting a hand to point at his shirt. "You're bleeding."

He spun around, where there was a patch of hair missing and a large, white square bandage taped over the wound. "Was. I'm fine now. Bit of an accident at work with a distraught patient."

"Someone attacked you?" I asked, sniffling and making my voice sound weaker.

"I'm fine." He sank into the couch next to me. "Big guy

didn't know who he was messing with. He hit me with a bedpan, I hit him with six milligrams of Lorazepam. We're even."

I feigned a forced smile, then let it slide away and, thankfully, he noticed. "What's wrong?"

I shook as I answered, using all my strength to call tears to the surface. "I... I lost th-the baby..." I watched his face closely, looking for a hint of the shock that should've been there. Shock at a minimum, though I would've preferred devastation. Much as I suspected, there was none.

"Oh, Alaina..." he said, pulling me toward him. I jerked back unintentionally, and he stared at me. There was the shock.

"Sorry, I'm sore." I ran a hand over my belly.

He nodded. "Of course. I'm so sorry. Is there anything I can do for you?"

"Just...stay with me," I whispered, curling up into the fetal position. I was doing a great job, if I did say so myself. "I don't want to be alone."

"Do you want me to get you anything? For the pain?" he asked. "I can get some Tylenol or ibuprofen...or something stronger." He raised a brow and pulled a small bag of white pills from his pocket. "They gave me these at the hospital for the pain. You may need them more than I do." I thought back to the small pill he'd claimed he'd left for my pain. The small, round, white pill with one letter and three numbers. From my research, I knew it was the second pill I'd need to take to complete my abortion. I assumed he'd crushed the first into the drink he'd left on my nightstand.

"No thanks. I've taken some already. I took the pill you left in the drawer for my headache, but it didn't do anything. You said it should've, right?"

He swallowed, unwavering in his sincerity. "Yes, that's right. It should've, but everyone's pain tolerances are different." He put a hand on my leg. "Are you...bleeding yet?"

I nodded. "It started last night."

He looked away from me, to the wall across from us. "I'm so sorry," he repeated, his tone so convincing it was scary.

"It's not your fault," I cried, rubbing a hand under my nose to keep a straight face, because we both knew it was. "It must've been the panic attack. I called the emergency hotline at the clinic last night. They said stress can do that in the first trimester."

He nodded, looking relieved to have a cause. "It's incredibly common." I stood up from the couch, hobbling down the hall. "Where are you going?" he asked, and I heard the couch shift with his weight as he stood to follow me.

"I need a drink." I reached the kitchen first, opening the fridge and grabbing the bottle of wine and the two already-full glasses from the top shelf before he caught up with me. I set them on the counter and pretended to pour them as he entered. The clear glass, grape juice, was mine. The blue glass, actual wine laced with a hefty dose of allergy medicine—the kind that made me extra drowsy —was his.

I lifted his glass, warming it with my hands before passing it to him. "Drink with me?"

He stared at me apprehensively. "I don't think I should. I can't stay long."

"You promised to stay," I argued, forcing a few new tears.

"I'll stay for as long as I can, but I'm on call. If I get a call for surgery, I have to go in."

"One little drink won't hurt," I told him. "You drove plastered the other night. A glass of wine won't get you buzzed. You know I hate drinking alone..." My chin quivered. *Please. I need this, Lukey.*

He sighed, giving in, and took the glass. "I'm sorry. You're right." He put an arm around my shoulders and took a drink of his wine.

I bent down, slinking out of his grip and holding my stomach with my free hand.

"What is it?"

"Just a cramp," I assured him, easing back up. "I shouldn't be on my feet for too long." Together, we made our way back into the living room. By the time we reached the couch, his glass was nearly empty.

He sat down first, and I sank into the couch next to him, watching as he stared off into space. "You okay?" I asked, taking a gulp of my juice. I was careful to stay far enough away that I didn't think he'd be able to smell the non-alcoholic grapes on my breath.

"Mhm," he mused, his eyes already drooping. It was entirely too early for the drink to have worked. It should've been a few hours before he began to feel sleepy. Had I accidentally overdosed him? I sat up straighter.

"You don't look so good," I said, touching his shoulder.

He shook his head, snapping out of the glazed look

he'd been wearing. "Sorry. Just a long night...and my head isn't helping." He downed the rest of his wine. "Or this."

"Maybe you should rest here for a while. Call in and tell them you can't come back. If you're hurt, surely they don't want you operating on anyone."

He yawned. "I can't do that. They did a CT at the hospital and everything's normal. Besides, it's you I'm worried about."

"I'm going to be okay," I vowed, meaning every word. He looked at me, his gaze somehow distant but concerned at the same time.

"I thought you'd be upset."

"I am, but there's nothing I can do, right? I'm trying to move on. To do better. Make better choices."

"Choices?"

I nodded, taking another drink of my juice. He reached for the glass, his motions sluggish. I pulled it away from him. "Go pour yourself more. This is mine."

He shook his head. Something was wrong, and it wasn't the medicine. There was no way what I'd given him had been enough to cause this reaction so quickly. I only wanted to get him to sleep, to give myself enough time to come up with a plan to have him admit what he'd done. To go to the police with the truth. I didn't want to kill him.

"How many of those pills have you taken?" I asked, staring at the pocket he'd pulled the bag from earlier.

He ignored the question. "What choices will you be making better?"

"Every choice I've made for the past two years," I said simply, taking another drink. He reached for the glass this time, one hand over mine. His grip tightened until I released with a shriek of pain. He put the glass to his lips and tilted it up. I swallowed, panic latching onto my bones and swirling through my veins as I watched him down the last of my drink. His lips curled, tongue running over his teeth as he narrowed his eyes at me.

"Meaning me?"

"What?" I tried to steady my breath.

"Meaning m—" He stopped, cocking his head to the side. "What was that?"

"What?" I asked again, scooting back from him and attempting to stand up.

"You weren't drinking wine." He looked at the glass, raising it to his nose. "Why did you lie?"

I pushed myself further back until my body was firmly against the arm of the couch. "I don't know—"

"Don't lie to me!" he thundered.

I whimpered then cleared my throat, regaining my composure. I wouldn't let him intimidate me. I stood from the couch, moving opposite him across the coffee table. "What? You mean you're the only one who can do that around here?"

"What the hell does that mean?" he asked, taking a step as he staggered then steadied himself on the arm of the couch.

"You tried to make me have an abortion!"

"I never lied about that!"

"About the pills? You forced one on me!" I looked to the space in between the couch cushions where my phone was set to record, hoping we were talking loudly enough.

His indignant expression changed. "You knew?"

"I'm not an idiot. I know what Tylenol looks like. And, with a little research, I found out what misoprostol looks like, too. Before I dumped it down the drain."

He growled and stepped toward me, his body swaying as if he were on a tightrope. "You knew all along? This has all been an act?"

"How could you do it, Lucas? You weren't even going to give me a choice? You were just going to kill our baby?"

"You can't do this alone. You have no idea what it takes to raise a child on your own. And I can't do it with you—" He stopped, pinching the bridge of his nose between his fingers. "I'm sorry, but I can't."

"I didn't need you to do it with me. I can handle it on my own. That didn't give you an excuse to murder my child."

He scoffed, blinking wildly, his eyes big and wide as if he suddenly couldn't see. "You can handle it on your own? Really? Have you seen this place? Where is the baby going to sleep? What are you going to do for money?"

"I can get a new place. I just sold a collection to a museum in St Louis. I can take care of this baby on my own, without your help."

"Until you sue me for child support."

"I'd have to admit I'd ever touched you for that to be the case," I spat. "And I'd never do that."

"You say that now," he said angrily, pinching the bridge of his nose again with a pained expression. "But it'll be different when the baby comes. I can't support you."

"I don't need your support!" I screamed, kicking at the table. "I need you to get the hell out of my house before I call the cops and tell them what you did."

"You wouldn't dare," he cried, stepping forward, a meaty finger in my face. "You hear me, you bitch? Don't you dare!"

I stepped back, crashing into the wall. "Don't talk to me that way!"

"I should've known it all this time. This was what you wanted. To trap me. To keep me here. Keep me stuck with you—"

I slapped him, the noise reverberating through the house. He fumed, his nostrils flaring with a heavy breath as his hands formed fists. He slammed his fists into the wall on either side of me. "You were good for a nice lay, Lainie. But even that got old after a while." He reared back, hawking spit in his mouth. His lips pursed and head still back, I watched him launch it into my face. I stayed steady, his warm, wet spit dripping down my cheek.

"Get out." My lips barely moved as I uttered the words.

He staggered backward, his movements unsteady as he turned around, shaking his head, the white bandage now a slight brown color, like dried blood.

I didn't say a word, didn't move an inch until he'd shut my door. I'd have to change the locks. I wiped the spit from my face with my palm, drying it on my shirt, and allowing the tears to fall—real this time.

This was over.

All of it.

I wasn't going to the police. I would never tell anyone what had happened.

I never wanted to see, hear from, or speak of Lucas Martin ever again.

CHAPTER THIRTY-FOUR

NAOMI

W hen the knock sounded at the door that evening, I jumped from where I sat on the sofa, the TV droning on though I was paying it no attention. I'd sat in silence, staring at the wall and waiting for the pounding at the door to let me know I was being arrested—taken to jail. That Lucas had told what I'd done. The notification that my life as I knew it was over, that everything good I'd done in my life had been undone by a millisecond's choice.

My arms shook as I walked across the room and into the foyer, wrapping the robe around my pajamas. I'd worn layers, feeling inexplicably cold, and I was intensely aware of Brent's gaze following me as I made it to the front door, peeking out the window to my right. The cop car sat in the drive. Two uniformed officers stood just beyond the door.

I looked back to him, the blood draining from my face. It was happening. This was real.

"Who is it?" he asked. Brent had helped me clean the

blood from the floor, he'd listened to me discussing all that had happened, and he'd reassured me that it was an accident, that I wasn't to blame. Despite his reassurances, we'd both just been waiting for Lucas to report to the hospital and turn me in. He had enough friends there, I had no doubts they could make the medical report say whatever he wanted. What better way to get full custody than to prove I'm an unfit, unstable mother and wife who tried to kill her husband? I swallowed, feeling bitter. It was such a good plan it made me sick. I'd handed him the keys to the palace. Was that what he was hoping for after all? Had he tried to agitate me into pushing him? I was the one who decided to climb the stairs, though... He hadn't led me, had he? I snapped back to reality, shaking my head at Brent with tears in my eyes. "I'm sorry," I whispered, no idea what I was apologizing for.

Brent stood. "Wait—"

My voice was shaky and hoarse when I opened the door. "Can I help you?"

The officers stared at me, their faces solemn. "Are you Mrs. Martin?" the first one asked, his deep blue eyes narrowing on mine.

"Y—" I cleared my throat. "Yes, I am. What's this about?"

"Ma'am, I'm Officer Bruce with the Davidson County Police Department." My blood ran ice cold, the room blurring around me. "This is Officer Lyons. Do you mind if we come in?"

"I..." I didn't know what to say. This was it. I was going to jail. Tears filled my eyes.

The officer cleared his throat. "Ma'am, there's been an accident."

Just like that, the blurriness disappeared, my vision and hearing returning to its original state. I brushed a tear from my cheek. "I'm sorry, an-an *accident?*"

"Do you mind if we come in?" he asked again. I was hardly listening, my thoughts racing. Brent was just behind me, his hand on the small of my back.

Becca. Becca was upstairs. Becca was safe.

My parents. My parents were in Bora Bora. They were safe.

It had to be Lucas. I looked back to Brent, who looked equally horrified.

"Please just tell me," I said softly, addressing the officers again.

The first officer nodded, straightening his posture. "Your husband was Lucas Martin?" he asked, and I heard it. *Was.* The word sucked the breath from my chest.

I nodded, my entire body numb. I felt certain I was going to pass out. "Yes," I squeaked out.

"I'm sorry, ma'am. There's been an accident on North Brumfield, near the Old Creek Woods. Your husband was the driver." He paused. "The accident was fatal..." He continued talking, but I was no longer listening. I fell to the ground, though Brent scrambled to hold me up. I didn't know what was being said. I didn't know what was happening or what I should be doing. What I did know was that up until that point, I was ready to never see my husband again. Now, given no choice, that fate was devastating.

Brent held me tightly, speaking to the officers as my

screams echoed through the house. I watched Becca's tiny body appear at the top of the stairs, watching it all unfold. I didn't hear what was said or what happened, but soon enough, the officers were leaving, the door was shutting, and Brent was on the floor with me, arms wrapped around me as my sobs carried through the suddenly too-quiet house.

He was gone.

My husband was dead.

My secret had died with him, but it felt like I'd died, too.

"What happened?" I choked out when I could manage to catch my breath. Brent shook his head, his jaw tight. I couldn't tell if he blamed me or not.

Was I to blame?

His only brother was dead. They weren't close, but he was still family.

I'd pushed him down the stairs just hours before his wreck, and Brent knew that. To my great relief, if he did blame me, he didn't move from his spot, and his arms remained around me.

"He's gone," he said softly. "We have to go identify the body."

The body. My chest went tight at the thought.

Because there was a body. Because he was dead. Because he was never coming back.

Because of me.

What have I done?

CHAPTER THIRTY-FIVE

CLARA

I rushed into the apartment, a mixture of vomit and blood down my shirt. I turned on the faucet, scrubbing the blood from the lines in my fingers, under my fingernails, up my arms. I stared in the mirror, at the blood speckled there.

Was it mine?

Or his?

There was no way of knowing.

I stripped my clothes away, knowing I'd have to burn them or dispose of them quickly. I had to get rid of any evidence. As my shirt passed over my face, I was overwhelmed with the smell again—burning flesh, vomit, blood. The sickening sound of metal crunching against wood. The deafening screams. I remembered the way he looked. His face, so much pain and fear. My heart had been pounding so loudly in my chest I was sure I was going to pass out.

It wasn't my fault, I tried to reason with myself.

It was an accident—a tragic accident.

But the police wouldn't see it that way. Not if they found out I'd fled. I pulled my pants off next, throwing the clothes into a discarded pile on the floor and stepping into the shower. As the water hit my face, I thought of him, of our many moments spent under this steady stream of water.

He was gone.

He was dead.

I fell to my knees without warning, my chest tight, and a silent sob escaped my throat. What had I done? What should I have done?

I was unable to stop myself from reliving the last moments of the life of the man I loved. The moments I knew I'd forever be haunted by and unable to share with anyone.

I hadn't wanted him to drive. It was why I'd followed. I'd wanted to protect him. I'd wanted to keep him from danger, but in the end, I'd been the most dangerous thing of all.

I had sat in my car, watching as he pulled up to an apartment I didn't recognize. It wasn't anywhere near his house, so I had to assume it was either a relative or a patient, but I didn't think he was stupid enough to go to a patient's home. It was strictly against hospital policy.

I guessed that didn't matter so much to him anymore, as he was—*we* were—planning to leave the hospital.

He was at the apartment for around an hour, me sitting in my car on the street, contemplating every bad thing he could've been doing in there. Perhaps it was his own apartment to escape Naomi, perhaps this was his mother's apartment, perhaps he'd kidnapped Becca, perhaps it was—

He had walked out of the apartment, interrupting my racing thoughts then, and I jumped from my own car, hurrying toward him.

He stopped, staring at me like he'd seen a ghost, then shook his head and hurried around to the driver's side. "What are you doing here, Clara?" He was angry. Agitated.

"I followed you," I said simply. We'd left things on such a good note, I desperately didn't want to ruin that. "I was just worried." I held out my hand for the keys. "Let me drive you home."

"I'm not going home yet," he grunted, pulling the car door open. "You should go back. I'm fine."

"You're obviously not. You're upset. Are you okay? Did something happen?" I gestured up to the building he'd left.

"I'm not upset; I'm fine." He tried to sink down in the car but stumbled.

"Luke, your head!" I shouted, grabbing at the back of his shirt and sliding my arm under his arm to keep him from falling.

"I told you I'm—"

I smacked my hand to the back of his head indignantly, and when he winced, I held it up, my palm covered in blood. "You're not fine. The stitches didn't hold. You're still bleeding, and we have to get you to the hospital."

He stared at my hand in panic, but it came across as a diluted version of panic, as if he knew how he was supposed to feel looking at his blood on my hand, but couldn't feel it down deep. "I'll go to the hospital after I get to the bank."

He made a move to get in, but I moved faster, shoving myself into the driver's seat. He groaned. "What are you doing?"

"I'm not letting you drive," I said firmly, arms crossed to show I was serious.

"You don't have a choice," he said, groaning as he bent down and scooped me up like a baby. He lifted my weight awkwardly, my legs banging into the steering wheel, head slamming into the ceiling, and half shoved me into the passenger's seat.

"What the hell?" I cried, holding my head and legs in pain. "Seriously, Luke?"

"If I wasn't fine, do you really think I'd be able to do that?" he asked, sinking into the driver's seat and starting up the car. I wiped the sweat from my brow, noticing the crimson stain he left on the headrest as he leaned back to buckle in.

"If you were in your right mind, I don't think you'd need to." I took in his appearance—wild, erratic eyes, flushed neck and cheeks. "Have you taken something else?"

He scoffed then attempted to pull out, but stopped to wait for a passing semi. "Of course not."

"Luke, I seriously think something's wrong. You could have a major bleed. We need to get you to the hospital."

He shook his head, pulling out, and I buckled up, suddenly fearing the worst that could happen. "You're losing a lot of blood! You're a surgeon, for crying out loud. How can you be so daft?"

He snorted, but he didn't look my way as he acceler-ated, turning onto the highway that led out of downtown.

"Luke, seriously, I don't feel safe right now. Some-thing's really wrong with you. You aren't thinking clearly."

"I'm fine!" he shouted, squeezing his knuckles around the steering wheel as he blinked uncontrollably. "If you don't trust me, you shouldn't have gotten in the car."

"I never said I don't trust you, just that I'm worried about you."

"Yeah, well, don't be. I can take care of myself, Cl—"

He stopped mid-sentence, yawning heavily.

"Are you tired? You could have a concussion! We have to get you to a hospital."

He looked over at me, still mid-yawn. When it ended, his forehead wrinkled. "I said I'm fine, damn—"

"Luke!" I cried, grabbing at the steering wheel as the car veered to the left and into the next lane, narrowly missing a silver car, its teenaged driver looking terrified. "Pay attention, would you?" We went around the next curve, his face a permanent scowl. "I really think you should pull over. I'll take you wherever you want to go, but I should drive. I understand you think you're fine, but you're obviously not. Whether you've taken something again, maybe a pill from your mom for the pain and it was a bit too strong or—"

"What do you think? You think I'm some junkie? You think I've just popped up to my mom the dealer and taken too many pills to ease the pain? I took a hydrocodone. One. I'm not an idiot, and I'm not high. You have no idea what I'm capable of handling. I didn't take anything more than what I needed!"

"I never said you did! Even if you took just an aspirin, if you have a bleed—"

"Damn it, Clara, I'm not an idiot. I'm a better surgeon than you are. I know not to take an aspirin while I'm bleeding."

I fought back bitter tears at his words. "Pull the car over, Luke."

"No."

"I said *pull it over!*" I reached for the wheel as we passed a patch of gravel on my side of the road, trying to steer us in that direction, anger radiating through me.

He tried to jerk it back toward him, fighting me every step of the way. I was looking at him, him at me, when the car crossed the lanes suddenly and left the road. We flipped, the side that he was on collapsing in on him until we landed upside down.

I stayed awake, aware of everything the whole time, though it all came as a blur. The car flipped again, moving at high speed until it slammed into a tree. Luke's body was smashed on impact, his blood splattering all over me. He stared at me, the scream escaping his throat was terrifying. My shin had smacked the dash, blood oozing down my leg. I unhooked my seatbelt, assessing the damage. His neck appeared broken, though it hadn't killed him. His chest had shards of glass in it, blood dripping from the wounds.

"Okay, okay, hold on just—oh, God..." I glanced down, where his pelvis had twisted, the hip bone visible from where I sat. His scream was animal-like as the pain set in. I closed my eyes, trying to think. "I have to call 911." I pulled my shirt off, trying to decide which wound to tend to first. "Put this on your neck," I said.

He stared at me, his eyes growing wider as his screams reached a peak. He couldn't move his arms. He couldn't speak. I knew it was over. I knew from my training there was no way we could save him. The floorboard was pooled with blood—his and mine, but mostly his. I leaned in to kiss his lips. "I love you," I whispered, tears trailing down my cheeks to land on his. I didn't want to leave him. I wanted to be with him until the end. But I didn't want to give up, either. With the right surgeon, the right medical team, enough blood... *No.* He'd still be paralyzed. He'd likely be dead either way. I pulled my phone from my pocket, staring at the screen. When I looked back up, I noticed the blown pupil. His brain was bleeding, like I suspected. It explained the slurred speech, the erratic behavior.

What do I do? What do I do?

I stared at my phone again, leaning in to kiss him one last time. I tasted the wine on his lips and assumed he'd lied about self-medicating more than he'd admitted, which hadn't helped the head injury. Of course, it had all been made worse by me grabbing the wheel.

I froze, squeezing my phone. Would they be able to tell it was what I'd done? Would I be blamed?

I looked at the love of my life. Was his life worth mine? No question. But would it be worth it if he wouldn't make it anyway? The decision was impossible, and I had mere seconds to make it.

I pulled back my shirt, and his eyes widened then fell closed. He knew what I was doing, but he couldn't keep his eyes open long enough to protest. I touched his hand. "I'll call for help," I promised. "I'm so sorry." I choked back tears as I pulled my shirt over my head. His eyes didn't open again as I forced my door open and climbed free, jumping down to the ground from the upright position of my side. I closed it back carefully, noticing the strong smell of gasoline. It hit me as I saw the clear liquid on the ground. I ran, pushing myself despite the pain in my leg, despite the pain in my chest—raw and emotional, telling me I was killing him. Telling me I still had a choice.

Telling me I was a murderer.

A coward.

I'd made it to the opposite side of the road when the explosion happened, the flames filling the air with the immediate smell of charred flesh, gasoline, and blood. I vomited in the wood's edge, holding my stomach with both hands as the tears mixed with the orange liquid.

What have I done?

CHAPTER THIRTY-SIX

ALAINA

Two days after the fight, two days after seeing Lucas walk out the door for what I knew would be the last time, I came across his face in my Facebook newsfeed.

He was dressed in a blue shirt and red tie, his white doctor's coat covering most of that. The headline caused my heart to skip a beat, my blood running cold.

Local man killed in one-vehicle crash on North Brumfield.

I clicked on the article. It had to be a joke. I stood, pacing as I read the two paragraphs over and over, skimming for the most important details.

"...car flipped three times...gas leak...no brake marks...explosion...dead on impact... Anyone with any information... Foul play has not been ruled out."

They were still waiting for a tox screen to come back. When it did, they'd find the alcohol, the large dose of allergy medicine...they already suspected foul play. Would that point them to me? Had he fallen asleep because of what I'd done?

I thought back to the pictures I'd sent him. The messages. *The tracking app.*

If I knew where his phone was, they could find me.

I shut my phone off immediately, picking up a paint brush and using its handle to smash it to bits. They couldn't pin this on me. I hadn't made him drive.

I'd made him leave, though.

If they found out we were dating—if he'd told his friends or coworkers—the police would come for me. I stared at the cracked phone on the table. Would that look more suspicious than the app?

I should've just deleted it.

I sat down, head in hands and elbows on knees, and rocked back and forth. I could tell them what he'd done, tell them why I'd made him leave, why I'd drugged him, but that would give me motive.

And the only evidence I had was on the phone I'd just destroyed.

I hadn't wanted him to die.

I just wanted him to pay for what he'd done.

No, don't say that.

Don't say anything. Lawyer up. You're innocent until proven guilty.

Would that make me look more guilty? I ran a hand over my stomach, willing myself to calm down. I couldn't have another panic attack. I couldn't.

If they came to me, if they found out he was with me either from his app or from his coworkers, I'd lie. I'd say everything was fine between us. *We were in love. I loved him. I'm devastated.*

At least that part wasn't a lie.

Lucas was gone.

It slammed into me—the realization. I'd wanted to leave him. To never see him again, but not like this.

He'd been good to me.

He'd loved me in whatever way he could.

I was still his fiancée as far as anyone knew.

Should I be planning his funeral? Or did he have family to do that?

I should wait, right? Until I found out more? Until I was contacted?

Would that be more suspicious? Should I be trying to call him?

We didn't live together.

We were casual.

The possibilities swam through my mind—every way to handle this. Every way to screw it up. I fought back the vomit rising in my throat.

What have I done?

CHAPTER THIRTY-SEVEN

NAOMI

Present Day

"So, is there... Is there anything either of you can tell me about the day Lucas died? Something to help put the investigation to rest. Something to explain to the police why he was headed that direction? Why he had a bag in the car? Why he didn't hit the brakes?"

"Put the investigation to rest?" Clara asked shakily. "Don't you want to know who did it?"

I swallowed. What did she know? "My husband died in a car crash. I don't think anyone did anything to him. Do you? It was just a terrible accident."

She dropped her gaze, staring at the floor. "I haven't spoken to the police. I don't know what they know or don't know. I just...well, I mean, I assumed, if they were still looking because they suspected foul play, there has to be a good reason. Isn't that what you said?"

I nodded, adjusting in my chair. "If you know something, by all means share it. I just don't want my family's grief to be dragged out any longer than necessary. My husband didn't have enemies. He was a good man, but he left behind a little girl who just wants to move on with her life. I can't have police in and out of my house, calling all hours of the day. I want this to be over. I want us—*all* of us—to be able to move on. Isn't that what we all want?"

Clara nodded, though it was obvious her heart wasn't completely in it. It was Alaina who met my eyes, hers filled with tears. "Do you think someone did something to hurt him?"

I shook my head, maybe too quickly. "I loved my husband very much. Though I hate what he did to us, I don't believe you two wanted to cause him any harm either. Did you?"

"Of course not," Alaina said.

"No!" Clara sobbed at the same time, wiping away tears from her honey-colored eyes.

"Well, then, it's agreed. None of us did anything and none of us knew about the rest of us. Though we can hate it now, we had no motive to begin with," I said, hitting it too on-the-nose, but I needed to know we were in agreement.

"Yes, of course," Alaina said. "I had no clue about either of you."

Clara nodded, though it was slower because of her tears. "I'm so sorry, Naomi."

I offered her a small smile, refilling my water and dabbing away a tear of my own. "Well, it's not your fault, is it? Lucas lied to us all. Cheated on us all. And now we're left to pick up the pieces."

233

"Do the police want to question us? Will they want to?" Alaina asked softly.

"I don't think so," I said. "As I've said, from what they've told me, I'm certain they don't know about Lucas' involvement with either of you. Unless you saw Lucas on the day of his death, I can't see how bringing you into the investigation will do any of us any good. I assume he worked a long shift…" I said, pausing and waiting to see if Clara would disagree. "I hadn't seen him that day at all. I believe he was just tired. Maybe he took a wrong turn. Do either of you have reason to believe otherwise?"

Clara twisted her lips together, and I watched her eyes narrow, could practically see the wheels turning in her head. When she spoke, she seemed conflicted. "No, I didn't see him that day."

"Me either," Alaina agreed. "We rarely saw each other, honestly. It was very casual between us."

"You were engaged," Clara pointed out, snapping Alaina's attention to her, and I did the same, noticing the way she was nervously rubbing her hands over her flat stomach. Was she nursing a bug, or was something else there beneath the surface? Perhaps it was just a nervous habit. But why was she so nervous? She didn't have the ring on anymore, I realized.

"I lied about that," she said sadly. "Because I thought you wouldn't let me see the casket otherwise."

I crossed a leg over the other. I should've been mad, but I was past that point. None of it mattered anymore. Clara seemed to agree as she sat quietly.

"It doesn't matter," I said, standing from my seat. "None of us are anything to him anymore. I don't expect

I'll have to see either of you again, and that's fine by me. Not to be rude, but we're connected by lies and a man who seemed to care very little about any of us. I'm having a hard time separating my loving husband from the man who could hide so much from me."

Clara stood too, setting down her drink. "Love makes a person do funny things." I stared at her, unsure what she meant, or why that mattered in this context. "Fear does, too."

"Were you afraid of Lucas?" Alaina asked, watching us both from where she sat in Lucas's chair.

"Never," I said. *Not until that last moment, but it was me I should've been afraid of.*

"Luke was nothing but kind and considerate toward me," Clara said. "And his patients." She smiled lovingly, staring off into space. "He was perfect."

"Except for the lying and cheating." Alaina stood up finally.

"Don't you think he's paid for that?" Clara asked.

"Was that what this was?" Alaina asked, her tone bitter. "Was it payment for all he's done? For all he'll continue to do to us for the rest of our lives? Are any of us planning to enter another relationship without a million reservations, thanks to him?"

She wasn't wrong, though I refused to admit it. I glanced down, where her hand rested on her stomach again, and when she saw me looking, she jerked it away.

"Are you pregnant?" Clara demanded, her voice powerless as she asked the question racing through my mind.

"Of course not. It's a nervous habit," Alaina said. "Are *you?*"

Though she wasn't asking me, I touched my own stomach, still flat, but not going to be for long. The test had confirmed the day after Lucas' death that I had another reason to be thankful he was gone. He'd never hold another child over my head. Never neglect another child who wanted his attention more than anything.

I glanced out the window, where Brent was playing with Becca and Rianne in the yard. He didn't know yet, just like I didn't know if the child was his or Lucas'. I wasn't sure if I would take the test to find out. Did it matter anymore?

"No!" Clara retorted to the question I'd forgotten Alaina had asked. "I'm too old to have babies. I'm married to my career. It's why I'd never get serious with Luke."

In the yard, Rianne bent down and scooped Becca up, tossing her in the air playfully. Brent watched from afar, laughing as he unpacked boxes of his tools into the garden shed. He was moving in slowly, though I'd never asked him to. It was an unspoken agreement between us—I needed him more than I wanted to admit. Once I told him about the baby, it would only be a matter of time before things would get even more serious between us. It was another reason I wanted the investigation to end.

Alaina sighed. "I should really be going," she said. "If there's nothing else you need to ask me."

I looked back at her, a question resting on the tip of my tongue I couldn't stand not to ask. "Did you love him?"

She started to shake her head, but stopped. "More than I should have."

"And you?" I asked Clara, studying her worn face. There was a compassion there I didn't see in Alaina.

"More than life itself."

I smiled, nodding slowly. I couldn't say that about my own husband. Of course I'd loved him, but not with the ferocity I saw in these women's eyes. I could pretend it was because we'd been together for so long, because we'd been through so much, because life had changed our relationship, but I couldn't shake the feeling that wasn't it at all.

I hadn't loved Lucas the way they had because he hadn't loved me in that way either. I was a project for him. Someone to save. Parents to impress. I was a way out of the life he'd had before me. A way to end the struggle.

"Thank you both for coming." The women stared at me with confusion, expecting me to say more. Perhaps I should've, but there was nothing left to say.

Clara squeezed my hand as she walked past, but Alaina didn't say a word. I walked them through the foyer, past the stairs, and out the front door.

"Goodbye, Naomi. Take care of yourself," Clara said, stopping to wave at the end of the walk. She wiped a tear from her eye.

"Goodbye," I told her, waving back and shutting the door as Alaina climbed into her car. When I turned back around, I was shocked to see Rianne behind me.

"What was she doing here?"

"Who?"

"That woman. Lucas'...er—" Her cheeks pinkened. "Well, his girlfriend, I guess."

I dropped my jaw. "Who?"

"The blonde," she said.

"You knew her?"

"She came by once, looking for Lucas. She thought you were his sister. I corrected her...I'm sorry, Naomi. I should've told you sooner." She paused, her frown growing more prominent, her eyes troubled. "Did you know?"

I shook my head, watching the sadness wash over her face even more. "It's okay, Rianne. I met her at the funeral and found out then."

"I should've told you—"

"None of it matters now," I said, patting her on the shoulder. "I just called her over to make peace. I can't hold a grudge for Lucas' wrongdoings."

She smiled, but it was half-hearted. "I can tell the police about her if you want. If that will help their investigation."

"Thank you," I said sadly. "But I don't think it's pertinent. I don't believe Clara meant Lucas any harm. His death was an accident." I started to walk away, but stopped. "If anything changes, I may take you up on that later."

She nodded seriously, studying my face too closely. "I'm going to get Becca some apple juice. Do you want anything?"

"Thank you. I'm fine."

I walked past her, lifting my glass of water and filling the empty one I'd meant for Alaina as I walked out the back door and into the yard. Brent's face lit up when he saw me. "How'd it go?"

"About as well as expected," I told him, handing over his glass of water. "I figured you'd be thirsty."

He took the drink gratefully. "You okay?"

I nodded. "They're innocent," I said. "And I don't think they suspect anything. I told them I wouldn't tell the police about them if they don't come forward about their relationships either. As long as they keep quiet, I have no motive. And whatever they know about our marriage, they have no reason to come forward if they don't want suspicion thrown at them."

He gulped down the water, dark patches of sweat on his blue T-shirt. "Uncle Brent! Can I work on your car?"

He chuckled, and we both turned our attention to Becca, who was carrying a blue hacksaw wrapped in a dark rag. "Whoa!" he cried, taking it out of her hands carefully. "How'd you get this?"

I moved to her, examining her hands. "Sweet girl, you can't touch Uncle Brent's tools, okay? Where did you find that?"

"It's what he used to fix Daddy's car," she said. "I want to fix a car like Uncle Brent!" She smiled proudly, reaching for the hacksaw, but he lifted it higher. "He said he could teach me!"

"When did he fix Daddy's—" I froze, staring at the panic in his eyes. He swallowed, resting his hands together in front of him. "Becca, why don't you go and see if you can pick Mommy a flower?" I pointed to a patch of purple asters next to the shed, not breaking eye contact with Brent.

"Okay!" She skipped away happily, leaving us alone.

"Brent, you didn't—"

He nodded, not bothering to deny it. "I couldn't let him hurt you."

"So you...you..." I sucked in a breath, trying to process. The memory returned to me—the evening on the stairs, while I'd been fighting with Lucas, Brent had taken Becca outside. I remembered the oil, then, that had been on his hands when we'd cleaned up the blood from the floor. I'd dismissed it at the time, unable to think about anything other than what I'd done. But I'd been worried about the wrong person.

"You wanted to leave him, but you were scared of what he would do. You were thinking he'd take your money, or, God forbid, Becca." He paused. "I was thinking he'd kill you."

My gaze shot back up to meet his, chills lining my skin. "*Kill* me?"

"I've seen my mother kill two men in my life, Naomi. Who knows how many more there were. My brother was no different than she was. You were in danger the moment you were no longer of use to him, just like I told you."

"But you don't know that for sure."

"I couldn't take the chance." He held the hacksaw out to me. "You can take this. Turn me in. It's still got my prints all over it, and I won't deny it."

"Why would you... Why didn't you just destroy it? I would've never known." I held the object flat in my palm, still letting what he was saying sink in.

"I had to keep it. If you were ever implicated, I had to have a way to prove it was me. I wouldn't have let you go to jail for what I did."

I touched my chest, tears brimming my eyes. "You let me believe it was me."

"I swore to you it wasn't," he said matter-of-factly. "I wanted to tell you…"

"But you didn't."

"I didn't want you to look at me the way you're looking at me now," he said, cocking his head to the side.

"Brent, I—"

"I won't apologize for what I did. I would do it again in a heartbeat. I learned how to love from a woman who wouldn't know the meaning of the word if it bit her on the ass, okay? So, I'm going to get things wrong. If this is too much for you, I understand. I'm not asking for forgiveness, or for you to understand. All I care about is that you're safe. And now you are." He watched me, his eyes dancing between mine.

The back door opened and Rianne walked out, Becca's juice in hand. "Everything okay?"

Brent nodded. "We're fine."

I shook my head. "Actually, no, Rianne, I need you to call the police."

His jaw dropped slightly, just an inch, then retreated. He made no move to stop me or defend himself. Rianne moved closer. "I'm sorry, what?"

"I need you to call the police after all. To tell them about Clara."

Brent's eyes went from empty to shocked. "W-what?"

"They should look into Clara. She may have been involved."

Rianne nodded. "Of course. I'd be glad to do it. Did you learn something new?"

Brent took hold of my arm. "Rianne, can you excuse us for a moment?" He led me inside. "Are you out of your mind? You can't give the police any more reason to dig than they already have."

"But Rianne knew about Clara. It pulls the suspicion away from you!"

He paused, staring at me with a solemn expression. Finally, he sighed. "You'd do that for me?" he asked, and I noticed a sudden glisten in his eyes.

"Look what you did for me," I told him, tilting my head toward my shoulder.

"I can't let you do this. I won't let someone else go to prison for what I did. Not you. Not anyone."

"You don't know that you caused it. It could've been his head injury."

"I sawed his brake line in half, Naomi. He had maybe a day before his brakes gave out completely. The head injury may have caused his driving to be worse, but I made the conscious choice to do what I did. If anyone is going to jail for this, it'll be me."

I choked back tears, placing a hand on my stomach. "I need you around."

"Then we stay quiet," he said, taking the saw from me. "We don't give them anything to work with. Let the investigation end."

I swallowed, realizing he wasn't understanding what I was telling him. Maybe he wasn't ready for that realization anyway. "Okay."

"What I did makes me no better than him. I don't deserve to be with you."

"You're right," I admitted. "But I don't care."

He lowered his lips to mine, the first kiss between us that wasn't wrong. "Neither do I."

I didn't know whose crime was worse—his or mine or Lucas'. I didn't know whose lie, whose action, caused my husband's death. What I knew was that answering that question wouldn't bring my husband back. I knew that Brent had done what he thought he had to, to protect me, just like I was willing to do for him.

I knew my husband wasn't innocent, because none of us were. We'd done the best we could with the cards we were dealt, to protect those we loved and to protect ourselves.

At the end of the day, a love like that was all I'd wanted.

Someone to make my eyes dance like Clara's and Alaina's had at the mere mention of Lucas.

Someone to love me no matter what.

Someone to protect me no matter what.

Someone to kill for me.

Turns out, I had that all along.

And it was all thanks to Lucas.

DON'T MISS THE NEXT
PSYCHOLOGICAL THRILLER FROM
KIERSTEN MODGLIN!

It was the trip of a lifetime...
until someone ended up dead.

Order *The Perfect Getaway* today:
mybook.to/theperfectgetaway

ENJOYED MY HUSBAND'S SECRET?

If you enjoyed this story, please consider leaving me a quick review. It doesn't have to be long—just a few words will do. Who knows? Your review might be the thing that encourages a future reader to take a chance on my work!
To leave a review, please visit:
https://amzn.to/2XMk79s

Let everyone know how much you loved
My Husband's Secret on Goodreads:
https://bit.ly/3gLuW3j

DON'T MISS THE NEXT KIERSTEN MODGLIN RELEASE!

Thank you so much for reading this story. I'd love to invite you to sign up for my mailing list and text alerts so we can be sure you don't miss my next release.

Sign up for my mailing list here:
http://eepurl.com/dhiRRv
Sign up for my text alerts here:
www.kierstenmodglinauthor.com/textalerts.html
OR text KM BOOKS to 31996

ACKNOWLEDGMENTS

I owe tremendous thanks to so many people for helping me to bring this story to life.

I have to start by thanking my amazing husband and sweet little girl—thank you for always cheering me on, for always encouraging me, for always believing in me, and for always being there when the good or bad news comes. I love you both more than I could ever put into words.

To my beta reader and closest friend, Emerald O'Brien —thank you for asking the hard questions, seeing the story through the fog, and helping me tell it in the best possible way.

To my editor, Sarah West—thank you for all you do. Your insights and ideas always help to bring my stories to a level I didn't think was possible. I'm so grateful to have you in my corner.

To my proofreading team at My Brother's Editor— thank you for being the final set of eyes on this story and polishing it to perfection.

To my review team, my Twisted Readers, and my fans

—thank you for showing up for yet another wild ride. I'm so thankful to have you in my corner, cheering me on, and loving my characters like I do. I'm forever humbled by your support.

To Rianne Doan—thank you for letting me borrow your name.

And finally, to you, thank you for purchasing this story and supporting my work. Whether this is your first Kiersten Modglin book or you've been around for a while, I hope this story managed to be everything you hoped for and nothing you expected.

ABOUT THE AUTHOR

Kiersten Modglin is an award-winning author of best-selling psychological suspense novels and a member of International Thriller Writers. Kiersten lives in Nashville, Tennessee with her husband, daughter, and their two Boston Terriers: Cedric and Georgie. She is best known for her unpredictable suspense and her readers have dubbed her 'The Queen of Twists.' A Netflix addict, Shonda Rhimes super-fan, psychology fanatic, and *indoor* enthusiast, Kiersten enjoys rainy days spent with her nose in a book.

Sign up for Kiersten's newsletter here:
http://eepurl.com/b3cNFP
Sign up for text alerts from Kiersten here:
www.kierstenmodglinauthor.com/textalerts.html

www.kierstenmodglinauthor.com

www.facebook.com/kierstenmodglinauthor
www.facebook.com/groups/kierstenstwistedreaders
www.twitter.com/kmodglinauthor
www.instagram.com/kierstenmodglinauthor
www.goodreads.com/kierstenmodglinauthor
www.bookbub.com/authors/kiersten-modglin
www.amazon.com/author/kierstenmodglin

ALSO BY KIERSTEN MODGLIN

STANDALONE NOVELS

Becoming Mrs. Abbott

The List

The Missing Piece

Playing Jenna

The Beginning After

The Better Choice

The Good Neighbors

The Lucky Ones

I Said Yes

The Mother-in-Law

The Dream Job

The Liar's Wife

The Perfect Getaway

THE MESSES SERIES

The Cleaner (The Messes, #1)

The Healer (The Messes, #2)

The Liar (The Messes, #3)

The Prisoner (The Messes, #4)

NOVELLAS

The Long Route: A Lover's Landing Novella

The Stranger in the Woods: A Crimson Falls Novella

THE LOCKE INDUSTRIES SERIES

The Nanny's Secret

Printed in Great Britain
by Amazon